LORD OF THUNDERTOWN

O.F. Cieri

A NineStar Press Publication

Published by NineStar Press
P.O. Box 91792,
Albuquerque, New Mexico, 87199 USA.
www.ninestarpress.com

Lord of Thundertown

Printed in the USA
First Edition
January, 2020

Print ISBN: 978-1-951880-21-7

Also available in eBook, ISBN: 978-1-951880-09-5

Warning: This book contains mentions of vomit, strong language, self-harm, alcohol use, death, gore, body mutilation, body horror, mention of discriminatory practices, mention of child abuse, internalized homophobia, mild use of homophobic language, and reference to anti-Semitism.

In the movies, Thundertown was depicted like a real town, with boundaries, Folk-run businesses, and a government. In real life, Thundertown was a block here or there, three businesses on the same side of the street, an unconnected sewer main, or a single abandoned building.

When an epidemic of missing person cases is on the rise, the police refuse to act. Instead, Alex Delatorre goes to Thundertown for answers and finds clues leading to a new Lord trying to unite the population.

No one has seen the Lord, and the closer Alex gets to him, the farther Alex gets from his path home.

Dedication

To Ken, for reading this book five times before there was
an ending

To Simi, for hyping something that didn't exist

To Claudia, I'm sorry it wasn't done in time to show you

Prologue

SAM WAS TIRED. All day long, she moved furniture in a small, dirty room in a warehouse in Brooklyn. She got on the train to go home. The conductor announced service delays, and Sam got as comfortable as she could in the glossy plastic seat.

There was no flash of lightning to signal a change. The insidious thing about the Aether was that humans were ill-equipped at handling it. Children had a better chance of being aware of it during a power surge, although they usually experienced it in migraines and blurred visions. The Folk handled the Aether best, and usually very judiciously, because the Aether was a force of nature that couldn't be reasoned with to respect private property or the sanctity of life. It activated when called and filled the parameters set out for it, and any gap in logic released a flood of unintended consequences. The only sign of something going wrong came from the lights in the subway shutting off abruptly.

Even then, Sam didn't panic. There were electrical surges all the time, and the lights usually came on in seconds. Instead, she remembered taking the subway with her elementary school class and shrieking with the other girls whenever the lights flickered, thrilled by the shock.

The train hit a hard bump, but rather than rocking back onto the track, the train lurched and tipped erratically. She couldn't see the other passengers, but she could hear the impact as they thudded against the far wall. Sam managed to hold her grip as a long-empty soda can flew past her head and empty sunflower seed shells rained past. Her heart gripped in her chest as she came face to face with the fact that she'd cast her shot and landed the one-in-a-billion chance to climb aboard a train as it tipped into the river. She was only surprised by how dark the sky was.

The Aether, according to scientific inquiry, does not exist. It can not be touched, seen, smelled, tasted or heard, nor can it be weighed or measured in any other way with tools. The Aether is completely undetectable by any means except the brain; and not clearly.

The train twisted, and so did Sam's grip. Her wrist popped as gravity wrenched it in an unnatural direction, and she fell, landing feet first on the seat she'd flown out of. Pain shot up her ankles, but the sharp jolt barely distracted her from the rattling of the carriage shaking across a hard surface. The high-pitched scream of sharp edges scraping across metal echoed throughout the train, and then suddenly ceased.

Humans have always shared the earth with Folk. There are records as early as the Kingdom of Ur, which mentions Other Lands that exist parallel to the common one. There are records as early as the written word of Great Beasts and supernaturally gifted nobility.

Sam turned on the flashlight of her phone. The windows were broken, and the foot of the train punctured through the floor near the door to the back. Someone was on the floor, trying to pull themselves up by climbing the train seat but not finding the friction, somehow. Another body sat upright, one shoe off. Slowly it raised its head and looked down at a hand that dangled lifelessly off their wrist. There was a guttural sob of pain.

When ancient kingdoms annexed new territory, they would often discover hostile members of the Folk. The ruler of the invading army would have to choose whether to destroy them, or bribe them. Soldiers throughout history have been immortalized for slaying Great Beasts in the service of their King, and similarly, simple farmers and fishermen were elevated to nobility by accepting the ruler's authority, and recognized as the Lord of the Forest, or Lady of the Lake.

"Are you ok?" Sam asked. The words slurred in her mouth. She couldn't be sure she was understood. She tried to stand, but her weight pitched in a direction she didn't expect and she stumbled. She pocketed her phone and dug out a small keychain light instead. More durable, she thought. Better use of battery power. "Are you ok?"

The Lords were meant to be the arm of the state regarding the Folk, any Aetheric or 'magical' phenomenon. However, reports of erratic or unpredictable behavior lead Government officials to tap more amiable outsiders for traditional Lordship roles.

It still sounded like she was drunk. There was a click behind her, and the rattle of the door between the train cars sliding open. The carriage was bathed in a dim orange glow. When Sam looked behind her, she saw the train conductor holding a construction lantern. She was an older black woman, gold braids disheveled.

"Is anybody hurt?"

None of this affects the quality of life for everyday Folk. Many preferred to live in the country where private property and building laws allowed them to maintain their own standards. While cities serve as hubs of commerce, the practical effect leaves many at the mercy of a standard of living, including enforced daytime activity, above-ground dwellings, little access to fresh or saltwater, and little tolerance for symbiotic parasite bonding. As a result, many of the Folk engage in creative means to maintain their health and well-being.

"Yeah--" Sam began.

A voice cut her off, shrill and panicked. "What's going on? What's happening? Why aren't we moving?"

The conductor raised her hand and tried to quiet the shouting passenger. "Calm down, please. I don't know, but before we find out, I want to get everybody off the train. Is anybody hurt too bad to walk?"

"No," said the person with the broken wrist. They sounded like they were in tears, muttering through chattering teeth; "No, no, no, no, no--"

"Good," the conductor spoke slowly and calmly. "Everyone, please follow behind me in an orderly line."

Thundertown is a well-known example, arising from an illegal settlement dug into an outcropping of Manhattan Gneiss in New York City. According to records, the Thundertown population was predominantly immigrant, with few English speakers in its first few decades.

The conductor walked down the aisle of the train, balancing against the wall for support. She led a trail of dirty and terrified people behind her, inching along as if huddling for warmth from the glow of the lantern. As she passed, Sam saw her holding a twelve-year-old girl to her waist, clutching her hand tightly. The small girl looked calm and supported the older woman's elbow as if carrying her gently above the crowd.

The City of New York has repeatedly dissolved the Thundertown settlement.

A pair of doors hung open a few carriages in. The conductor dipped her light outside and pressed her toe down, testing to see if it was safe to leave. She clutched the side of the train door as she lowered down, her foot swinging out blindly for something to anchor itself to. Slowly, she touched down on something, and slowly she shifted her weight off the train and onto the ground beneath. The ground was flat, uniform, and unremarkable.

Unfortunately, the area is too well-known to remain closed for long.

There were no train tracks.

Chapter One

ALEX DELATORRE LIVED in a loft with an ecosystem. Ants and roaches marched around the building, eating leftovers from the human tenants, while spider beetles and silverfish ate their refuse. Mice ate the roaches, and the goblins ate the mice, leaving behind a single pink foot, or a small coil of dark-blue intestine.

There was a factory below the loft. They didn't care about the roaches or the mice, but the goblins could destroy their equipment if left uncontrolled. The goblins were attracted by the warmth, the electric static in the air that gathered soot in clumps, and the ozone smell of hot machinery. They liked how many intricate little parts came off the equipment and the exotic texture of plastic, wire, and rust on their teeth. To keep them at bay, the manufacturing company paid a local Lord from the Night Court to come by once a month to destroy their nests and refit the protective Aetheric design around the work floor. The design was a complicated piece of architecture that required a lot of math to accurately map as many environmental details as possible, for the Aether was a blind, senseless force of energy that would fill any overlooked gap at random. All members of the Folk could see the Aether, which could protect them from backlash; if not, they could heal deeper wounds. The Lords were, theoretically, better educated in Aetheric design, and authorized to handle Aetheric issues.

Alex knew for a fact that the neighborhood was officially protected by a different Lord than the one the factory paid. He'd heard the Lord of the area was like a skeleton covered in thick, wiry gray hair and deeply wrinkled pink skin. According to legend, he never blinked or smiled. Regardless, the loft above the factory couldn't afford to pay fealty to a Lord, and since the loft wasn't built for housing, it didn't come with a standard repulsion ward. Instead, tenants stuck paper wards around the apartment, which were supposed to alchemize trace mineral components in the air to mimic silver, which didn't hurt the goblins but kept them at bay. At night Alex heard the sound of drywall crunching as the goblins tested the boundaries of the wards, chewing on the wires and tearing up insulation.

Alex sat at the kitchen table with three job applications open in one browser window, and the Paraterrestrial Bureau of Collaborations homepage and the Night Courts and Day Courts in another. He ground a curly strand of stripped-white hair between his teeth to the rhythm of the machines downstairs.

The kitchen was a small, windowless room. Once, the loft was another factory floor full of machines; then it was converted into storage. The management company in charge of the building found it more profitable to rent out the loft for parties in the nineties' than leave it vacant. Eventually, the event planners rented out rooms to pay for the space, and the room partitions became smaller until all that was left was a claustrophobic hallway and the dark kitchen around the table.

Alex's roommate, Nails, was making coffee in the sink. The kitchen was in perpetual midnight under the unnatural glow of the fluorescent light, an outdated fixture left over from when the floor was a factory.

Alex stopped at an email with the subject "I'm not dead."

From: Stereophonic0406@gmail.com

im not dead

send me ur number new phone

He held his breath. Samantha went missing in August, and now, they were running out of days in September. Big, strong Sam, twice Alex's size in both directions, who didn't say much and was struggling to get a tattoo career off the ground. All her things were still in her apartment when her roommate let Alex in to check. Her posters, her shoes, her album collection, and one long row of dark-colored fitted caps were all lined up the way she left them. Her clothes were in plastic boxes, her favorite chains piled on top so she could sift through them in the morning. Nothing seemed to be missing: no last trace of conflict alerted him to danger.

When he went to NYPD, they refused to help him, and when a month passed, they told him his only choices were to go to the courts or seek counseling.

Alex snatched up his phone and dialed the number at the bottom of the message. The phone rang four long times and then sent him to the voicemail box. He hung up and called again. This time, Sam picked up on the first ring.

"Who's this?"

It was her. All business, voice pitched low. "Sam? What the fuck— Where did you—"

Nails looked up sharply from the sink.

"Sam?" he repeated.

"Is this Chelsea?" Sam asked.

"It's Alex," he said. "Where are you?"

"My place."

"What's up with Sam?" Nails asked, pulling out a chair at the table.

Alex covered his free ear and turned away from Nails's prying stare. "You're *where*?"

"Home."

"Where've you *been*?" he cried, slapping Nails's hand away when he reached out to take the phone.

"I got snatched up," Sam said. "Been stuck in Thundertown."

"What Thundertown?" he demanded. In the movies, Thundertown was depicted as a real town, with boundaries, Folk-run businesses, and a government. In real life, Thundertown was a block here or there, three businesses on the same side of the street, an unconnected sewer main, or a single abandoned building.

"A big one."

"What the fuck does that mean!?" Once upon a time, recently enough for Alex to remember, there was a Thundertown uptown in an abandoned limestone quarry as big as anything Hollywood could imagine. It had been shut down by the City years earlier.

"I wanna talk to her," Nails demanded, reaching for the phone. The harsh white light above them cast sharp shadows over his face, like a character in a noir film.

Alex dodged him. He was tired of fishing for answers out of her over the phone. "Stay there. I'm coming over."

He hung up and turned to Nails. "Sam's back."

Nails had large eyes, which gave his face a permanently startled appearance. Actually startled, he looked confused. "*Sam*? Holy shit. Where's she been?"

"Thundertown," he said, getting up from his chair.

"Uh," Nails said, as Alex entered their shared room. "That's gone."

"Yeah, that's why I'm going over," Alex said as he closed the door to change. When he came out, Nails was chewing very slowly on a dry bagel. He was tall and skinny, with heavy bags under his eyes, stubble over his scalp and down his chin. Sam was the first person to tattoo him on his eighteenth birthday. Alex watched him sob the entire time, swearing he was never getting another one. For two weeks, he picked at it, flaking off skin, watching it heal. When there was nothing else to peel off, he went to Sam for a halo of nails across his back, from penny nail to railroad spike.

"Hold on," he said, his mouth full of bagel. "Before we go anywhere and do anything, I wanted to bring up some of the concerns I have. So like the cops said there was, like, no chance she was still alive, right?"

Even after hearing her voice, his words made Alex's chest tighten. "The senator thought there was."

Nails raised his hands. "I hear that, and I want that to be true, but on the other hand, that might not be her."

"Who else would it be?"

He wagged his head and spoke carefully. "I'm thinking you heard so much about Thundertown that you went out to get the Lords involved, and maybe instead of Sam, we got back—maybe—something else?"

"Like what?" Alex demanded.

He grimaced. "Maybe that's a mimic."

That was one option too many. He shrugged on his coat. "I can't think about that right now. I'm going to go find out."

Nails only stared at him, unblinking, before rushing to grab his jacket and follow Alex out the door.

NAILS HAD A Metrocard but had to open the gate for Alex. Fortunately, there weren't any transit police to ticket them. As they sat on the train, Alex found himself distracted from the conversation by his own reaction to Sam's reappearance. His stomach hurt, his teeth were grinding, but he wasn't sure what to name the negative feeling rolling in his gut. It was something between frustration and disappointment, as if he was angry that Sam's return was so simple and quiet. She re-appeared the way she disappeared: without ceremony.

He'd gone to the police, but they turned him away with nothing but a suggestion to go to the courts. The website for the United Court Assembly of the Tristate Area was an ancient, flat website with only enough bandwidth for a long list of names and phone numbers, half of which seemed to be disconnected. There was some sort of Non-Government Organization designed to assist communication between human and Folk governments, and they had a modern website, complete with working links, called the Bureau of Paraterrestrial Collaborations. On their website, they helpfully explained that people could live in the jurisdiction of certain Lords, but not pay for their protection. Most Lords expected something for their services and saved their time for people who could provide something in return. When Alex went by, Sam's roommate couldn't tell him if she paid fealty.

Nails brought him to the Lord of the block he grew up on, the King of Battle Row. The City allowed developers to turn his neighborhood into the entrance to the Holland Tunnel, and he accepted the project in exchange for a decimal fraction of the annual toll. Now he held court in an old bar near the highway, lit by mounted TVs and passing car headlights. The furniture was faded and scratched, seats filled with old men watching a game on TV.

The King of Battle Row was barely four feet tall, with long limbs, a red face, and hair so thin and colorless it seemed to pick up a tint from his skin. He spotted Alex and Nails around the bottle's neck and wrinkled his face into ugly fury. "What do you want?"

Nails gave him a broad smile, the one he used when he was deeply uncomfortable and desperate to hide it. "Hi, Battle Row. My name is David Kaczorowski. Do you remember me? My mom and I used to pay you fealty—"

"Until when?"

Nails halted and stammered. "Uh, about four months ago? We were on—"

"Why'd you stop?"

"We lost our house."

Battle Row took a thoughtful sip of his drink. "Want me to fuck up the building management?"

Nails hesitated for only a beat. "I mean, yeah, but that's not what I wanted to ask you about. I wanted to ask you about a friend of mine who's missing. The cops told us—"

Battle Row wrinkled his pale eyebrows. "What does that have to do with me? Did the friend ever pay me?"

"No?" Nails guessed.

"Then what should I care?"

"But, I mean, *I* pay fealty—"

"You did. I'd do you a favor, but that doesn't make your friends my business," Battle Row grunted. He turned away from them and went back to his cards.

Nails gave Alex a helpless smile.

Alex took that as his cue to step forward. "Could we pay you?"

Battle Row took a drink and played another card without looking up. "It's not my business."

"But paying you is business," Nails wheedled.

Battle Row put down the bottle and turned his stool to face them with a loud, rusty squeak.

The bar was instantly silent. Everyone in their private conversations at their isolated tables froze, and next to Alex, Nails took a half step back. Battle Row's face was twisted, cartoonish, and red as a stoplight. He was so ugly and so visibly furious, it struck Alex as funny.

Battle Row held the silence for one long breath. "My business is my business, not yours. I never want to hear suggestions. I'm not helping any of your friends, or relatives, nor anyone who used to pay me however many months or years ago."

"But it was only—"

"Did I ask you a question?" Battle Row barked. "I don't know who you think you are, but you better learn your manners."

Nails's mouth clapped shut.

"God damn kids," he muttered, bending back over his cards.

NEXT, ALEX TRIED to ask the Courts directly for help. By then, Sam had been missing for two weeks. The court building was deep in the Wall Street area, in a nest of streets tied like string around property lines that no longer existed, but he found it eventually. Both the Day and Night Courts shared the same ancient, crumbling brick building, wedged between glass-fronted offices. Behind the wooden door was a narrow front room, decorated with a thin red rug, a brass umbrella stand, and a dry plant. There was a plastic window on the other end of the wood-paneled room, where a small, wrinkled woman with tall, furred ears, directed Alex through a door.

He expected to find himself in a lobby, but the door opened instead on a dark-green hall with a skylight that didn't fit in with the colonial stone structure. He followed the hallway around the corner to a long line of teller booths with copper grates. Aside from the one teller in the far corner, the room was empty. The lone employee gave him paperwork to sign and directions to a third stop.

He followed a tight flight of winding stairs around the corner to a locked office door with a wooden bench outside. He took a seat and finished the paperwork while he waited.

As time passed, he wondered if they knew he was there. He knocked until the curly white head of a small man appeared at the door.

"Sorry, we're closed."

His stomach dropped. "*What?*"

The small man shrugged. "Ask the front desk for a timestamp and we'll see you first thing tomorrow morning."

"I can't come back tomorrow!"

The small man sighed. "If you don't want to wait, go to the Night Court."

He walked back through the dizzying maze of doors and hallways as the lights in empty rooms clicked off behind him.

By then, the sun was gone, and the wind was sharp enough to cut through his Carhartt jacket. There was already a small line of people on the steps, all dressed in a mix of found objects and elaborate tailored clothing. The man in front of him had a cloak of black feathers, the woman before him a knitted shawl over a puffy longcoat. He put up his hood, put his hands in his pockets, and settled down to wait.

The Day Court staff trickled out in groups, talking, listening to music, pointedly ignoring the line growing on the steps. Other Folk walked in behind them, juggling their breakfast. The Night Court opened a few minutes later with no announcement or ceremony, and the line inched forward even as Day Court employees continued to hurry out.

The space where the Day Court window used to be was replaced with smooth wood paneling, and the Night Court window sat on the opposite side. Alex lingered as long as he could by the radiator vent until it was his turn to approach the receptionist's window. She directed him through a new door, which led to a wide set of tiled stairs. At the top was another line of tellers behind dark oak booths with copper piping, but this time, the room was packed.

The line was full of people with hooves, horns, fur, scales, feathers, and a broad shape covered in long, dry branches. Alex's eye kept lingering on an enormous troll carrying her head in an embroidered straw basket. When it was his turn, he got new paperwork and directions through yet another doorway.

He found himself on a huge work floor with wide windows that showed a view of parking lots, single-story warehouses, and, most unnervingly, the very Manhattan skyline he should have been part of. Office workers swarmed in and out of the rows of desks without looking at him. He tried to stop one, but they twisted away, muttering something like, "Be right with you."

When his turn came, a small, green person with a back like a softshell turtle shuffled his papers to the sound of his complaint, signed a sheet of paper, stamped a second, and then handed him the pink copies. He stared at the pink sheets for a long time without understanding the gesture, until it dawned on him that he was finished.

"What happens now?"

"We'll call you," the softshell turtle said.

A FEW DAYS later, the Night Court wanted Alex to clarify some details by providing paperwork he didn't have—or at least didn't recognize by name—so he returned empty-handed. They explained the paperwork they'd asked for would prove if he or Sam had a Clan's sponsorship, or paid fealty to a Lord within the Night Court. Because neither of them did, their case would be left up to anyone who would be willing to take it. Alex got a call within the hour and eagerly gave them his name and information. Common sense sobered his enthusiasm when they asked for his credit card information.

HE HAD BEEN tempted to give up when a friend recommended Senator Loisaida. Alex never heard of a Lord using the title of Senator before, but after speaking to her, he learned she was the first Lord in America to be elected. Her title was symbolic, a gesture meant to invite political rivals to political debate rather than territorial battles. She was known in Alex's circle as the Lord who helped the squatters prove the property holders of their buildings were negligent back in the nineties. She took his paperwork, copied it, and gave it back; that was all.

Now, without ceremony, explanation, or announcement, Sam was back—a phone call and a train ride away—as if nothing went wrong.

They arrived at her building, an old tenement designed to hold people like produce, stacked on top of each other. Nails leaned on the doorbell until the intercom snapped to life, buzzing like a swarm of flies.

"Let us up," he shouted.

There was another burst of static, with a high lilt at the end like a question.

"It's Dave and Alex. Let us in!" Nails said. The door unlocked with a different quality of buzz, and after four flights of stairs, they reached Sam's apartment. She answered the door in frayed pajama pants and an ancient Madball hoodie, holding a pint of ice cream.

"What's good?" Her hair was the longest Alex had ever seen, laying in ringlets on her forehead and peeking around her ears.

"What's *good*? What happened?" Alex cried.

"I got snatched up," she said.

"You said that already. It doesn't mean shit. What happened, Sam?"

She sucked on her spoon. "I was going home. Then the train stopped. We were sitting in the dark for about a half hour. No emergency lights, no flashlights, no cellphones. Then Cassandra—she was the conductor—went through the train with one of those big-ass flashlights you see them carrying around, unlocked all the doors, and got everybody out. We only figured out we weren't in the City anymore when we realized there were no tracks. Cass was the only one with a real light. Me and a few other people had those little LED flashlights you keep on your keys. Some people used their cell phones, but those burn up power real fast. The first night was bad. Quiet. Dark. Empty. We slept on the train and waited to hear something, or see something.

"The second night was worse. Big fight broke out. Some people wanted to stay, some people wanted to turn other ways. Cass said she thought maybe that was a subway tunnel a long time ago, or some other kind of construction site, but it didn't look like anybody had been down there in years—which meant nobody was probably going to come. So, I went with the group that was leaving. Cassandra went with her radio, looking for a signal, Rich came 'cause he couldn't sit still, Eric and his wife didn't want to stay, and Leticia came because— I dunno. Maybe she was scared.

"We found this bum camp, and some of us thought the people in it were human. I didn't. We passed it and kept walking until we found a settlement and figured out how to buy stuff. Bought some lights, food, a map, and made it to the second settlement. That's where I got this."

She reached into the neck of her sweatshirt, pulled a chain over her head, and gave it to Alex. The chain was cheap, like something out of a vending machine, with a thin disk of hammered silver hanging from it, etched with an incomprehensible Aether matrix in cuts thinner and more fluid than ink.

"What is it?" he asked and then stopped his hand as the light caught on a cloudy shape under the figures. On one side of the rim was a little line of indents from the original printing that still said 1927. Now he recognized George Washington under the Aether matrix, stretched from ponytail to chin into a flat, formless cloud. The coin was a quarter, hammered smooth and fitted to wear on a chain.

"I gave them one of my tattoos for it," Sam said, pulling up a pant leg to show a pink patch of skin.

"*Sam!*" Alex cried, aghast.

"At least they healed you up," Nails muttered.

"We got attacked on our way over, and I figured protection was a good idea. Couple of people got weapons. I thought that was kind of stupid. Those Folks *are* weapons, and any kind of knife or sword they carry around is a threat or an ornament. There were little towns, like a block or two long. There was a lake. Rivers. No trees. No sky."

She fell silent. Her gaze dropped to the ice cream carton in her hand, which she scraped with her spoon half-heartedly.

"But where were you?" Alex asked again.

She shrugged. "Thundertown."

"But where?"

"Underground."

Alex scoffed, furious with her for not answering his questions.

"How'd you get back?" Nails asked.

"Some big dude grabbed me," she said, spreading her arms wide to show the scale. "Huge. He lay down and stuck his arm through the cave to grab me. I thought the design on my necklace was busted, then I'm on my roof, and the sun's coming up."

"What the fuck," Nails muttered.

Sam clenched the spoon between her teeth and dug a long plastic container out from under her bag. When she opened it, the salty smell of swamp water filled the room. Alex and Nails both pulled their collars over their nose.

"What the fuck is that?" Alex cried.

"My gear," she explained, pulling out a dirty backpack. "Didn't have time to clean it."

One by one, she emptied each pocket. Her gear was full of unremarkable things: napkins, coins, matchbooks, promotional keychains shaped like bottle openers, books, leftover food packages, and dirty laundry. Most of it was tied up into plastic bags to keep it dry and clean, but as she dug, she found water stains and set them in their own pile.

She shook her head as she worked. "It's a fucking shitshow. My roommates rented out the room. Place was full of cans before you showed up. I paid up until the end of the month; then I'm out."

"Wait, what? Are you moving? Are they throwing you out?" Alex asked.

"No. They've been chill. I'm going back."

Alex blinked blankly. From the minute he woke up, his day had been a roller coaster ride while he ran behind it, trying to climb on. "Why?"

She looked at him like he was an idiot. "I can't leave them."

"Who?" he asked.

She gestured vaguely, looking as confused as he felt. "My friends. The others. The ones still there."

He pinched his eyebrows. "Sam, calm down. OK? Stop for a second."

She paused, waiting.

"I want to talk to Loisaida before we do anything—the Lady we went to when you went missing."

"But I gotta get started."

"How were you going to get down there?" Alex asked.

"Take the subway," she said slowly, as if she wasn't sure how to recreate the trip.

He took a deep breath, satisfied. "We'll start with taking it to the Lady."

Chapter Two

LOISAIDA'S OFFICE WORKED on Night Court time, which was open at five in the evening until nine in the morning for everyone on a nocturnal schedule.

Alex, Sam, and Nails met her on the sidewalk as she was opening the office, juggling her purse, keys, and coffee. She was little and pretty, with big eyes and a helmet of permanently straightened hair cut short around her chin.

"Sorry I'm late," she babbled. "Come in, sit down—I mean, when we get upstairs. It's on the fourth floor."

She took them up the elevator and into her office. There was one large wooden table in the center and a few smaller ones pushed against the wall, facing away from one another. There was a dead plant in the corner, a microwave, water cooler, coffee machine, and filing cabinets. Stacks of cabinets in a variety of colors and sizes lined the back wall; old and new, broken and sturdy, but all of them spilling paperwork.

The senator went to the back of the room, leaving her bag on the counter. "What can I do for you?"

Alex stepped forward. "We're following up on a missing persons case."

She turned on her laptop. "Last name?"

"Delatorre. Two r's."

She tapped it in, chewing on her bottom lip. "Alex, right? You submitted the case on behalf of a friend. And she should be back by now? A neighbor identified her from a poster."

Sam's eyes widened. "That was no fuckin' neighbor."

Loisaida gave her a passing smile, mind clearly elsewhere. "Are you Samantha? Nice to meet you. How are you?"

"That was your guy that shook me up?"

"A former tenant of the neighborhood, but I wouldn't call him *my* guy. He saw the alert for a missing person and responded as he saw best—although I recommended alerting the police. I'm sure it was shocking for you."

Sam's face fell as she spoke. "What about the others? Tici, Rich, Horace, Cassandra?"

Loisaida blinked expressively, which broke something in the air around her. Alex felt like his vision was shifting as he looked at her, almost like being exhausted and trying to read. Her eyes seemed to grow in her head like a corrupted image file.

"Others?" she repeated.

"You think I was the only one there?" Sam demanded.

Loisaida raised her hands in the air to signal surrender. "Alex told me that you were missing. He didn't say anything about others."

"He doesn't know them," she said, then waved her hand, refusing the conversation shift. "Wait a minute; your guy, the guy, where did he find me? Where was I?"

"I'm not sure; I didn't ask. From what I've gathered, I think it's one of those old construction sites some Folks are living in, or maybe the basement of an old building. There is so much space in New York that it's impossible to keep track of. How did you end up there, anyway?"

"One minute I'm on the subway, the next the subway's in this big cave." Sam cried, frustrated.

The gentle smile on her face disappeared, and her eyebrows sank. "Can you explain a bit more?"

Sam, clearly annoyed that she had to tell the story again, gave her a version even shorter and sparser than the version she gave Alex and Nails. When she was done, Loisaida grew very quiet. Her eyes drifted down to the desk in front of her and focused there.

She propped her elbows on the table and steepled her fingers. "That shouldn't happen."

"True," Nails agreed.

"Are you going to help me or what?" Sam snapped, cramming her hands in her pockets.

Loisaida sat at her desk in thought for a few more minutes, then stood with a smile. "Absolutely. I want you to begin by sketching out all the details you can about the friends you made there."

Sam's eyebrows furrowed. "Right now?"

"No, of course not. Take my card and make an appointment."

Sam tried to argue, to press her for more details and more answers, but she responded so quickly and so tactfully that they found themselves back on the sidewalk before they could form a rebuttal.

Sam squinted back up at Loisaida's fifth-floor office, then at Alex. "Is she gonna help?"

He shrugged. He only knew her marginally better than Sam, although he was surprised by her lack of trust. Sam frowned, turned, and started walking.

"She'll probably put up more signs." Nails said, trailing behind her.

"Yeah," she said. "I'm gonna go uptown to check out that old entrance."

Nails stopped walking so abruptly that Alex walked straight into him.

Alex shoved him aside. "To Thundertown? Isn't it closed?"

"If it's closed, it's closed," she said. "You wanna come? I got some flashlights."

THE THUNDER TUNNEL started as a limestone mine in Dutch-controlled Harlem, but as residential homes crept into the industrial zone, the more the mines posed a hazard. People lived in the tunnels, although no one knew how many, or for how long. By the early 1810s, there were reports of employees going into work and never coming out. Usually only one or two disappeared, except for one busy workday in 1821 when a whole work floor vanished.

Several Lords offered the factory their protection but broke their contracts one by one. The Tunnels, full of hidden chambers and warring factions, were impossible to regulate. When the employees brought portable, personal protection, the Folk in the Tunnels broke their equipment. The quarry was abandoned in 1850 and songs, stories, and rumors sprung up around it.

The City shut down Thundertown before Alex and Nails were old enough to see it. Thundertowns were security blind spots where no cop or surveyor could go without permission. They never saw anything except what they were supposed to see.

The group stopped by Sam's house before taking the subway to 181st. The train rattled past stations, leaned over sharp corners, raced out of the tunnel, and climbed elevated tracks. As they sped over rooftops, they watched the traffic below. Peering into bright windows for mere seconds, they caught glimpses of people in their homes or offices, a dance school frozen in place, and a woman leaning out a window to smoke. When the conductor announced the last stop in Manhattan, they got out on a platform high enough to feel it in the chill of the air. From the platform, they were level with the lights of apartment buildings and could look down the lamplight-studded hill at rows and rows of closed shutters, rattling in the cold wind.

The light from Sam's phone lit her face as she looked up the address to the old entrance. On the other side of the hill was a steep cliff of gray stone surrounded by the highway. They crossed the ankle-high divider between the sidewalk and the brown grass and walked into the legs of the steel girders holding the buildings above them.

Alex felt a mixture of excitement and apprehension. He always wanted to see the Thunder Tunnels, but he was still too young to feel safe navigating the road to it when it was open.

"What do you think is there?" he asked.

Nails shrugged, skimming the stone cliff face with his flashlight to read the graffiti. "Maybe nothing."

"Maybe Thundertown," Sam said.

Alex's body felt like it was any other night, but his mind was buzzing. They snuck out on rooftops for fun, catching the front door with a warm smile behind people not afraid of strangers. They circled blocks looking for an entrance into boarded-up megaplexes, they climbed fire escapes and fences with hammers hidden in their coats to pull up plywood coverings, rip through construction scaffolding, or pull chains loose enough to slide under. This was different; when they broke into old movie theaters or abandoned strip malls, they took great care to not disturb anything or anyone. They were going into Thundertown to disturb it.

The mine was surrounded by a chain-link fence far away from the highway. The original mine entrance was gone, and all that remained was a brick building with boarded-up windows on a grassy hill. Most of the bricks were worn down, leaving a honeycomb of the mortar between them. The longer they looked at it, the more he felt it should not still be standing.

Sam found the gate locked with a loose chain. Alex and Nails slid through easily, but she needed to jerk the fence until it bent to squeeze through. They climbed the slope of broken stones that was once a set of stairs up to the doors of the factory where a modern fence was awkwardly installed into the leaning doorframe. The doors were sealed with a bolt and several Aether designs that were too complicated for Alex to read. One of them seemed to alchemize wood to concrete; another one he could clearly tell made a loud noise if the bolt was broken. A reflective sign on the gate read, "NO TRESPASSING BEYOND THIS POINT." Sam went to the window and pushed wooden boards until she found a loose one, and they climbed in.

As soon as they swung over the frame, the sounds of the highway were muted, and the cold wind died. Inside the decaying structure, the wandering bricks were plugged with moss and vine. The first floor was like a terrarium with vaulted ceilings laced with pipework and full of bare, light-starved plants. Nails clicked on the flashlight and shined it over the walls, following vines through the wooden boards and bricks.

It was a little space, barely more than six connected rooms. It was hard to think of it as the heart of a mining operation. Alex wondered what remained of the company that built the factory— the long scrolls of peeling wood?

The patches of old print on the floor? Did they lay them, or did someone after them repair it? The factory was far from a sealed time capsule. The beam from Nails's flashlight passed over trash in deep puddles, a torn mattress, a pile of wooden pallets, a dirty jacket, and an electric fan.

"Are you sure this was the entrance?" Nails asked from a different room, leaning through a collapsed wall to talk.

"Yes," Sam said. "Came up here a few times back when it was open. I remember stairs."

Alex pointed his flashlight at a collapsed pile of wood that formed a ramp to an empty window. The air was hot and humid in the rooms at the back, and much darker. The roof was more stable, and the cliff was keeping the wall upright. Rainwater pooled in corners, trembling with the force of their footsteps. Hunks of wood were frayed like old cloth, and whole floorboards were reduced to nothing.

Suddenly there was a crash and Nails shouted. When Alex and Sam whipped around to point their flashlights on him, he was up to his knees in a hole. It had been camouflaged by pulped and matted garbage, but it didn't look as if Nails punched through the floorboards. Instead, it seemed like he'd put his foot in a hole cut a long time ago.

Sam and Alex both dropped their flashlights and grabbed his shoulders, steadying him enough to help him climb out.

"Are you OK?" Alex asked.

He stretched and bent his knee, hissing through his teeth. "I'm fine."

"I think you found it," Sam said, pointing her flashlight down the hole. Inside was a stairwell carved straight into the ground out of weather-smooth stone leaking cold air into the hot room. Sam put one foot down the hole and wobbled. She tried another step, found her balance, and slowly lowered herself down.

"Sam," Alex warned.

"I remember this," she said faintly. She steadied herself on the wall and took another step down.

"Careful,"

"I'm fine, Mom," she called up from the bottom of the stairs. Hesitantly, he knelt down, clapped his hands on either side of the hole, and lowered himself down. His heels kicked against the smooth stairs, and he stumbled but caught himself on the cold and slick ground. Nails dropped down after him, landing in a squat. He took the flashlight out of his back pocket and turned it around the room.

"I guess this is the mines," he said.

Chapter Three

THEY WERE IN a low cavern thick with cold and slippery deposits of mineral, like a forest of dirty ice. Pillars and vines of bulging crystal stood as if frozen in the act of bubbling over. When Alex touched one, it was slimy. He wiped it off on his vest.

There was a path worn through the ice, beaten into a cloudy wave by the rough outline of feet. Sam stepped into someone else's footprint and walked hesitantly forward.

"We should probably not leave the entrance if we don't know where we're going." He shouted after her.

"So stay there," she shouted back

"We should have brought some string," Alex muttered. Nails gave a non-committal shrug and chewed on a tab of skin hanging off his thumb. "Don't do that. Your hands were all over the floor."

Nails went right on chewing.

There were two small lights a few feet above the ground just outside the beam of his flashlight, but they disappeared like a candle flame when he pointed it at them. As they walked, the path got wider and flatter. The uneven waves of ice turned into a thin, glistening sheen on solid rock, and then became a clear road leading deeper underground. The tunnel was wider as they traveled further inside. Loops of dripping crystal pulled off into other directions as the path lead them further down. Gaps high in the rock seemed like windows high over their heads.

They saw a small fire up ahead and two small figures sitting in front of it but didn't stop to talk. Not much farther on they passed a short, dark shack with voices coming from inside but didn't stop there either. Farther up the road were the remains of structures long abandoned, the foundations of small buildings, the marks of fire, and the splintered legs of furniture.

"Is any of this familiar?" Alex asked.

Sam shook her head.

The path they chose veered right and followed a concrete wall, fitted with a metal door frame. There was no door, just rusted hinges covered in ice. Sam stepped over the lip without hesitation, but Nails stopped to look the doorframe up and down with heavy judgment. It was much smaller with a higher ceiling, but in contrast to the naturally-formed ice caves behind them, the tunnel was a perfect rectangle. Along the ceiling under predictable bulbs of mold and ice were empty light fixtures.

The ice was even thinner behind the door frame, enough to feel the pebbled ground beneath them. They followed the hallway to a set of stairs, at the base of which was another metal door, silhouetted by light like a copper frame. Warm air escaped through the cracks melting the last thin layer of ice on the stairs and walls. When Sam tested the knob, loose but still holding on to its setting, she found it unlocked.

"I don't like this," Nails said.

"I'm just going to look," she said. "What could happen?"

"You really want me to answer that question?"

She made a sign for quiet and cracked open the door enough to peek inside. Whatever she saw inside didn't alter her expression an inch, but it made her stand aside and push the door open. Behind it was another short flight of stairs tall enough to block their view of the floor above it, and beyond that were the sounds of a crowd walking, talking, and occasionally shouting.

Carefully they all crawled up the stairs, leaning on each other's backs so they could poke their noses over the top stair. Above them was an enormous concrete dome over a wide, flat floor covered in tables, tents, and stalls. Figures milled between them arguing and laughing or passing by to reach one of three tall, peaked hallways in the back. The solid walls, the point on each arch, and the old, orange glow of the halogen lights made Alex think of a government building buried deep underground.

Sam's expression went from cautious to critical as she cast a second glance around the market, and then with two slow rolls of her shoulder, she shook them off and rose.

"Looks like the place."

The old light brackets were too dim to see by. Most light came from lamps set up on stalls. There were modern lanterns, old oil-burning lights with warped glass, naked bulbs burning on tables with no wire or plug, and a few stalls that seemed to be backlit by nothing at all. Goods were arranged on booths, under tents, spread on carpets, and hawked out of carts. There was too much to remember; a woman selling birds with curved nails as long as her arm, a square silhouette ten feet tall, and something in a rug dragging roots instead of feet.

"Well, shit," Nails said. "Now what?"

"I'm gonna ask for some kind of information broker," Sam said.

"What if they don't have information?" Alex asked.

"Then I don't pay them."

She went to the stall closest to them and asked the man behind it if he knew any information brokers. He only shrugged, so she went to the next stall who waved her away rather than answer. She went to the next one and the one after that while Nails and Alex watched. It was clear that nobody wanted to talk to her, a human who didn't want anything they were selling, aggressively asking questions in a Folk market that had been shut down once already.

Nails muttered something about her technique and went to another aisle, striking up a conversation with the first person who made eye contact with him. They talked and laughed for a while, but when he asked for an information broker, they abruptly turned and walked off. Alex watched him jog to the other end of the aisle to ask someone else, and the scene repeated. He began gently and friendly but ended up with nothing.

Confused, Alex picked another aisle and walked over to a stall. This one seemed to be selling turtles in small plastic carry cases. He turned his head in feigned interest until the stall owner came over. She was wearing a bad glamour of a woman with red hair and lips but without any of the texturing of real skin or hair. It made her face look like an airbrushed mask and her hair like a twisted copper sculpture.

She smiled back and laid one unwrinkled, hand-shaped plastic mold on one of the top cages. "They can be very good pets if you take care of them right."

"I'm not actually looking for a turtle," Alex admitted. "I'm just kind of overwhelmed."

"First time here?" she asked, smiling when he nodded. "Take your time."

"Actually," he said, as off-handed as he could manage. "I'm looking for an information broker."

With the heavy glamour over her face, it was hard to read her expression, but the way she looked him over was chilly. She turned her back to him. "I don't know. Sorry."

He left the stall, sucking his teeth. Through the crowd, he could see Sam working her way, table by table, through the market while Nails flitted around with a fake smile and a spark of desperation in his eyes. Alex looked up and down the aisle he was in, trying to find a person who wasn't busy or visibly tense. He spotted another stall run by a small figure wearing an enormous hat with holes for their blue ears and marched over to them.

Over the next hour, he managed to speak to a handful of people, who all had more or less the same reaction as the red-haired woman. Others were more interested in how he made it there, while some people treated him like an undercover cop, or, at least, like someone who could spread rumors a cop might overhear. All of them seemed to think he was a dumb kid. When he finally got too hungry and frustrated to ask again, he found a stall selling overcooked noodles for a dollar and sat against a wall to eat them. Nails found him there, just as worn out and hungry, and bought his own container. Soon they were all sitting along the wall, shaking hot sauce into tasteless broth.

"So," Nails drawled, licking hot sauce off his fork. "*Now* what?"

"You know what, why don't you tell me?" Sam snapped. "Why don't it be your turn to come up with answers? Now what do we do, Fingernails? Huh? What do we do now?"

He frowned into his soup. "This was your idea. We both told you it was stupid."

"I didn't hear suggestions from you."

Alex jumped in before the argument could escalate. "We made it, we're here, but if there's a guy, no one will tell us. So, seriously, what do we do, and when do we give up?"

Sam pointed her chopsticks down the three tall, arched hallways. "We didn't try there yet."

Nails followed her chopsticks and made a face. "How far in are we going? I got work tomorrow."

"You work at night, Nails."

"All I'm saying is that we don't need to go stall to stall to hear the same answer over and over again. I'll do *some*."

She rolled her eyes. "We each pick a hallway."

"And then we each come back at the same time," Alex added.

"When?"

"An hour," Sam said. Nails let his jaw drop. "That's what I said, an hour."

"All right, all right. An hour," Alex said. He figured Nails would give up first. Since Sam knew them well, she would follow up on their two hallways as well as her own— which gave him a half hour to walk his hallway then another half to rest.

When they were done eating, they split up. Alex's entrance was cluttered with litter and litter pickers but wide and clean on the other side. The first stall to catch his eye had its own light show with a scrolling banner, three neon signs, and a beer clock, while the table was covered with the same cheap jewelry people could buy on a card table anywhere. Alex kept himself from pulling a face. So far, the famous Thunder Tunnel market was just a really big flea market.

He walked, ignoring the booths. At the end of the hallway, he found a spiraling set of stairs leading down into an even deeper depth. He wondered, not for the first time, what this much basement was doing in Harlem. He took two hesitant steps down, backed away, and then leaned over the railing to look down. All he could make out was an intersection full of foot traffic through the bloom of lights, and he wasn't willing to risk getting any more lost than he already was. He made his inquiries with a handful of booths in the alley and slowed to a stop at a clothing rack to browse. Outside the hallway, where the crowd was thicker and the lights a little brighter, he found their noodle stall again and sat against the wall to wait for the end of the hour, mildly surprised Nails wasn't there already, waiting for him.

He asked a person for a spare cigarette, who turned out to be eager to sell him a pack for some of the studs on his vest. He fished a few loose ones out of his pocket, tore the cellophane off the pack, and settled down to wait.

The crowd thinned and then thickened as the tides of shoppers went by, groups passing by, breaking up, and then forming again. The market was calm around him, but he felt an uncomfortable awareness as he watched the crowd. It felt like he was in a room full of people pretending not to watch him. The nicotine covered his throat like dirt, but he ignored it and tried to blow smoke rings into the lights.

When he looked out at the crowd again, he saw a large, hairy shape standing still in the crowd. His skin crawled. The alarms that steered him faithfully through the turbulent waters of life were tripped by that tall shape that seemed to be watching him. He flicked away his cigarette and walked into the thickest knot of people nearby. He made his way to the hallway where Nails was supposed to be and worked through the crowd to find him. At the end of the hallway was a small locked door. He jerked on the handle without any success and turned away to worm his way back towards the market.

At the head of the tunnel, the tall silhouette stood out above the crowd. Alex felt a buzz of nerves shoot up his spine and dived out of traffic. He landed in an empty booth with a startled-looking shopkeeper.

Alex hurried over to her. "Excuse me! Did you see another human come through here?"

The stall keeper shook her head.

"You sure? He's white, really skinny, and bald."

She shook her head again.

"Thanks," he muttered and crossed the aisle to another booth. "Excuse me, did you see a white guy about my age and my height, who looked real tired come through here?"

"Yep," the stall keeper said.

"Did you see which way he went?"

"That guy there took him," the keeper said, as he pointed to the large shape trying to wade its way towards them. Alex watched the shape come, frozen. There was no way, he thought, this could be real. He must be mistaken.

The shape came close enough for Alex to make out that it was covered in thick, dark fur with a nose like a nutsack and round, shiny eyes. It smiled with porous teeth and lips, like stones in a sponge. He realized in a rush of cold how exposed and vulnerable he was. The hairy thing tried to stretch across the crowd to reach him, and without thinking, he dove under the table.

The merchant shouted and shoved aside boxes to grab him. Alex squeezed through the table legs into the next booth, shoving storage out of his way and crawling out into the open in the next stall. People were shouting, but he ignored it. He ran abruptly out from under the table and crashed into a man selling umbrellas. Alex caught his fall on the other side and took off running. He crossed the whole length of the market in a flurry of shoulders and outraged pedestrians until he was back at the entrance. When he looked back over the heads of the crowd, the silhouette was too far to see; for the moment, he had lost them.

Alex sat down to breathe through burning smoker's lungs. He needed to check up on Sam, but the solid concrete bunker, though wired for light, was not satellite accessible. He peeked above an overturned trashcan and at the three tall hallways through the crowd. The large figure was caught in traffic and struggling to squeeze past the exit. They craned their head to look inside the next hallway, allowing the current of shoppers to draw them in.

Whether Sam was there or not, Alex had to find out. He didn't have a change of clothes to alter his silhouette with, but he did his best by covering his vest with his coat and tucking all his hair under his collar. The third hallway was as long and dark as the others, but part of one wall had caved in completely and created a new ramp for customers to use.

He turned to the first stall that caught his eye. "Did you see a big, angry white lady?"

The merchant paused. "You mean a human? I saw a human with short hair come through here. Black baseball cap and flight jacket. Couldn't tell if it was a lady."

"That's her."

They shook their head. "She was asking a lot of questions."

"Yeah," Alex said impatiently.

"She went outside." They pointed at the hole in the wall.

He groaned and climbed the hill of broken concrete. Sharp edges cut his palms. There were yellow lanterns mounted somewhere in the darkness above him, and the crowd below seemed thick with wispy shapes that fled from his flashlight. As he looked back at the crowd in the market, he saw a huge shape pulling itself through.

Alex blindly grabbed the nearest person. "Excuse me! Did you see somebody? A human with short hair? Black hat? Black flight jacket?"

Their shawl ripped in his hand. The creature let out a rattling hiss and scurried straight up the slope of the wall. Behind him, gravel crunched under huge feet, and he took off down the tunnel.

The path weaved erratically. He tripped over a short flight of stairs and tore through rotten patches on his jeans. He got up and kept going through a forest of stalactites when it curved to follow the wall.

When he finally slowed down, he was in a new area of the cave network covered from floor to ceiling in roots. There were no lights. He sat on a knot of old tree root and panted for air until his head throbbed. When his breathing finally slowed, he listened for footsteps behind him. The cave was silent except for the sound of dripping. His hands and knees were cut to ribbons, and his pants were unwinding to thread.

Alex shakily got to his feet and shined his flashlight around for another exit. Maybe, he thought, there was a way to loop back to the market. Maybe he could find that staircase he saw earlier. As he was scanning the wall, his flashlight illuminated two lamplike eyes across the cave.

He froze, turned off his flashlight, and listened. Stones broke off the ceiling and fell to the floor somewhere ahead, as something climbed toward him. He braced himself as his mind raced for some kind of plan. He had nothing but his flashlight—maybe he could blind it?

Alex waited. The sounds of rock breaking became more frequent and irregular, as if there was more than one pair of footsteps. The noise got louder until he felt like all the walls around him were being crunched underfoot. He squeezed his flashlight so tight the grooves in the grip cut into his skin. When should he do it? What should he wait for? What if it was too late? What if the thing was on top of him?

Alex flipped on the flashlight and shined it on the troll from below, casting deep shadows across its face. The two pupils in its bright, glassy eyes shrank to pinpricks. Alex pushed off the side of the wall and scrambled for balance on his hands and knees. The troll reached out blindly, but he ducked its arm and came up behind it. He turned and ran with his flashlight swinging by his side, casting long, spinning shadows all around him.

Alex had barely made it to the other side of the cave before the beam of his flashlight disappeared, and the taste of cloth filled his mouth. Something heavy pressed down on his shoulders. Blind and frightened, Alex flailed wildly.

He gasped for breath, tasting the cotton bag on his tongue. Suddenly, in the stuffy, close darkness of the bag, he felt his vision split like each eye was sliding in a different direction. Heaviness sunk into his limbs. He tried one last time to buck the strange, hard little thing on his back. Alex had a sudden vision of himself, like a flash in the dark, waving his arms in slow motion with each position of his arms arranged like a fan at his sides. He focused on this image as he tipped forward and turned helpless somersaults like an astronaut in space.

A slow, quiet voice in him was still trying to analyze the situation; was this a date-rape drug? If so, how did he ingest it? In the noodles? He sailed away, stuck on the mechanics of drugging a box of watery noodles, with a fever image of a hand shoving timed-release capsules into congealed noodles on repeat. The capsules got bigger and harder to work with as the hallucination dragged on. He could feel that smooth, tacky surface between his hands, growing bigger than a cup, bigger than a football, trying and failing to push them into a box of noodles, as the tasteless hot water splashed everywhere.

The darkness rocked and stripped away to reveal blinding light. Alex heard people speaking around him, but his head was ringing too hard for him to listen. He wrapped his fingers around his wooden seat to steady himself. The storm in his head ebbed and flowed, but at a lull, he planted his feet and swung the chair. The momentum knocked him off balance and sent him crashing into the wall.

The talking stopped.

He struggled to untangle his legs and banged into the walls around him. He drew his knees to his chin and stared out through the slats.

He was in a small office, with eggshell-white walls, a desk, a computer, and two heavy oak chairs. The troll was looking down at Alex with disappointment. Clinging to their shoulder was a small, boney body with a turtle shell and a skullcap full of water. There was a man behind the desk with his chin straining to jut out of the collar of his suit, and his jowls pooled around his shoulders.

Chapter Four

THE MAN SIGHED. "What have I told you about the burlap sack?"

"It's not our fault," said the troll. "They keep running from us."

"So you threw them in a sack and dragged them here?"

The troll fell silent.

The man in the chair turned his attention to Alex. "I'd like to apologize."

Alex spotted a door to his right, jumped up, and grabbed the doorknob. On the other side of the door were Nails and Sam, sitting in a pastel-puce waiting room with tight, frightened expressions. Nails jumped to his feet when he saw Alex.

The door closed firmly on its own and locked as Alex grabbed the knob.

"Anyway," the man in the suit said, ignoring Alex as he tried to pry the lock open with his EBT card. "I can't pay you for any of them."

"They were lost and we found them," the little body cried.

The man in the suit sighed and rubbed the bridge of his nose for a long time. He addressed Alex again. "If you'd be patient, I'll be with you in a second. You don't have to destroy my door."

To the troll and its passenger, he said, "It's not your job to ambush targets. Don't expect money for any clients you bring me in a sack."

"That's not fair!" The troll roared and slammed a fist as big as the man's head into the desk. The wood made a deep crunch underneath.

"Not fair to who?" the man asked, pointing at Alex. "Them?"

The troll turned to go, brushing Alex out of their way. Nails was waiting on the other side, ready to force his way in as the door opened, but the troll pushed him back like it was keeping a cat from running between its legs. When the door shut behind it, the room was quiet again.

"Are you"—The man squinted at a paper on his desk.—"Aaberg, Ralph?"

"No," Alex said.

The man nodded as his collar bunched the loose skin at his neck, and he ran his finger across a column on the page. "Abajian, Megan?"

"Where am I?" Alex asked.

The man gave Alex a withering stare. "Are you Megan Abajian?" he repeated.

"No. Where am I?"

The man sighed and let the papers in his hand fall slack. "You're in my office."

"And who are you?"

The man had to stop and consider before he could answer. "I think you should call me the Kijkaan."

"Great. Let me out."

The man made a gesture of acquiescence.

Alex immediately jumped to his feet and ran for the door.

"I won't hold you against your will, but we're not finished here," the man answered.

He ignored him and ran to Nails and Sam. They jumped up as soon as they saw him.

"What happened?" She asked.

"That big, hairy motherfucker knocked me over the head and carried me here." he gasped, feeling breathless.

Nails nodded. "Same with us. What happened to the stupid herald shields?"

"I don't *know*," Alex groaned. "Where are we? Who is that? What's with the names he keeps reading out?"

"I don't care," Nails said.

"I feel that," Alex agreed.

"Me, too. Let's get the fuck out." Sam said. They rounded the first corner they saw and found a line of locked office doors. They turned around to pick a different direction. Alex looked over the white stucco walls and the line of locked doors and could feel the illusion cast around them like an itch at the back of his neck.

At the end of the hallway, they picked a new direction. They found a stairwell behind a door with one light bulb burning over the landing between the darkness above and below. They climbed up the old, rusty stairs, with the iron arches and spirals of floral decals, although the flowers were mostly rusted over, or snapped off. When they reached the top, they found it bricked shut.

Nails's breathing was an uneasy wheeze. Under Sam's flashlight, he glowed pale, sweating and shaking.

"Do you need to sit down?" she asked.

His eyes wheeled around the stairwell in terror. "Not here."

They lead him back down the stairs with the circle from their flashlight weaving across the stairs. With a groan, Nails pushed past Alex and Sam and stumbled to the bottom of the stairs. He landed on his hands, shaking, and rubbed sweat out of the hollows of his eyes.

He nodded down the other flight of stairs. "We going down next?"

"We could wait," she offered, but he shook his head.

"I want to get the fuck out of here."

Sam and Alex walked ahead, shining their flashlights on every step. Leaves of rust broke off under their hands. Alex caught his thumb on a sharp edge and checked to see if the skin was broken. Nails suddenly grabbed the back of his jacket and pulled, knocking them both over. Alex threw out his hands to catch himself, and the beam from their flashlight somersaulted over the edge of the handrail.

"Nails!" He started to curse but stopped when he realized there were no more stairs beneath them. Just a bent, rusty handrail descended down.

Nails gagged and pressed his sweaty forehead against the cold brick wall. "I need water."

"I guess we have to go back," Alex muttered.

THE SMELL OF mold was stronger in the hallway, the lights brighter, as if they had walked onto a fully lit movie set. The lights seemed to drill right between Alex's eyes, the way he used to feel around Aetheric designs as a kid. Back then, headaches like these happened frequently, but as he got older, they were increasingly rare. The last time he'd felt the weight of so many conflicting Aether constructs squeezing his skull was during a class trip to the Aether exhibit at the Natural History Museum.

Sam found a water cooler in the waiting room and pressed the nozzle. Nothing came out but the faint smell of moss. Further down the hallway, the door to the office swung open to invite them inside.

Nails shook his head. "No. I'm not going in there."

He took a seat close enough to the door to see inside while they caught the door before it could swing shut and propped it open with a chair.

The man didn't make a remark but tapped the edge of his stack of papers and began again. "Are you Aaberg, Ralph?"

"What's that list?" Sam asked.

He looked at her with a touch of surprise. "We've taken a commission to bring the lost back to the surface."

"We're not lost," she said at first, then amended her statement. "Not like that. We came here on purpose."

A sigh whistled through his nose like steam released from a high-pressure valve. He spoke slowly, "I want to be sure I can't cross your names off this list. Are you sure you don't want to listen to the full list to see if your names are here?"

"No," Nails said.

"You could have been added by accident."

"*No*," he insisted.

Sam signaled for silence. "How many names are there?"

The Kijkaan glanced back at the cabinets against the wall.

Sam's eyes narrowed. "Hell no."

"It wouldn't be quick, but it is important."

"Why are there so many names?" Alex asked.

"There are a lot of missing people. More, I think, then I have listed."

"I'm looking for some people. Could you tell me if they're on there if I only have first names?" Sam asked.

The Kijkaan gave her a dry look. "I could find them provided the two of us built a more substantial profile on them. I don't want to assume your budget, but it could end up being very expensive."

"What would you charge me?"

"We can settle on a fee if you want."

"No... I mean... what do you want to be paid?"

His eyebrow twitched. "Money."

She wet her lips. "Let me take a card."

One stood up in the cardholder on the desk for her. She put it in her wallet.

The Kijkaan leaned back in his chair. "If you don't want to participate, you can go back to the Surface as soon as you like."

Nails, listening at the door, snapped up. "Now."

"I think you deserve to know where you are and why you were brought here."

"*I don't care*," Nails shouted back.

The Kijkaan ignored him. "You're probably already aware that the city enforced an integration program after the attacks on the World Trade Center. For the past few years, our community has respected the program, but as these things tend to, the loss of our neighborhoods is beginning to affect us. Some of us have different needs than our Human neighbors; some of us can't be exposed to daylight, others need the freedom to regulate our environment in specific ways. The list goes on. Human society doesn't work for those of us who don't have the build or mobility required to live in the city—which is ridiculous when not even humans come in the same shape every time."

"What does that have to do with us?" Sam asked, but he ignored her and went right on talking.

"Despite all their best intentions, many of us can't follow the guidelines the city has set. And the ones who went back to their homes in Thundertown are in an uncomfortable legal position. The only solution is to offer the city complete transparency; by putting Thundertown on the grid, helping the people who want electricity to sign up with Con Edison, establishing a safe garbage disposal, and giving an accurate census of how many people are here. Then, each citizen can keep their independence and enjoy life in a modern city."

Alex's limited experience with Thundertown made him think transparency would cost more than trash pickup and electricity if the sight of three kids made half the market pinch their nose. How would all those trash pickers handle a Health Inspector?

"Who cares?" Nails asked again, which summed up Alex's feelings. Attaching a new, smaller city to a much larger city didn't matter to any of them.

The Kijkaan gave them each the same strained smile and continued on. "The problem is the scale of the project. Combining the needs of our population with the needs of the City government has never been done—well, not successfully. Today, we're fortunate to have a Lord who is dedicated to Thundertown's development. We'll finally be represented in the city's courts by a Lord who is principally responsible for its upkeep and who can delegate tasks to the best possible candidates. Not only will this generation of Thundertown have the protection of a Lord but also a chain of command available to listen to their petitions. It'll be easier than ever to finish construction with a team working together."

The smell of mold tickled the back of Alex's throat and made him cough. He did his best to wet his throat and clear the thick, sandy feeling. "Are you selling something?"

The Kijkaan answered with a bark of laughter. "If I was, I would say it didn't need selling."

"Then what's your point?" Nails demanded.

The Kijkaan leaned forward and propped his elbows on the table, which spilled the neck meat tucked at the back of his collar. "My point is that the Lord has finally isolated the problem with a city government establishing guidelines for a population used to living underground. Plans to unify the two populations have historically failed because they tried to enforce rules on people who could dig away from them. What we propose is a connected network of tunnels to give the people in Thundertown freedom of mobility they've never experienced before. For the first time, anyone can visit any other part of Thundertown at any time of day without ever leaving the Tunnel System. So many people moved to the city for accessibility, that even if we do lose a handful of residents to dead-end warrens, we can't lose enough to stop it!"

He paused to gauge their reactions. Whatever his expectations were, it was clear by his expression that they didn't live up to them. Alex and Sam weren't listening anymore, and Nails never started. He pushed on anyway.

"Construction is minimal. We're incorporating as much preexisting subterranean real estate as we could find. For example, where we are now was originally part of a department store. While my office is expanding the project, we're establishing a connection to the outside."

"And these names, where are people going?" Sam asked.

The Kijkaan's smile wavered. "We're not sure."

She sucked her teeth derisively. "How are people getting into the sites?"

The Kijkaan showed her his teeth in an expression too flat to be a smile. "They must have their ways."

"I was lost for a while. Me and my whole train that I was on. We weren't spelunking."

The Kijkaan shrugged. "Like I said, there are a lot of possibilities to choose from. It's possible that someone outside the train purposefully brought all of you to one of our sites. Or a rider on the train performed, or maybe was wearing, a design that reacted badly to one of ours."

Her eyebrows furrowed. "You telling me these designs are so unbalanced anybody could tip 'em?"

"They pass all government regulations for public Aether use, but even the best Designs can be buggy," the Kijkaan said quickly.

"But you can let us go, right?" Nails demanded.

"Absolutely," he promised.

Nails sprang out of his seat. "So let's be out."

Sam remained in her seat and narrowed her eyes. "You heard of Representative Loisaida?"

"Lo-ease-side-a?" the man asked.

"She was big in the squatting movement in the '90s," Alex said.

"Squatting *movement?*" he repeated. "I'm sorry, where was this?"

"Downtown," Sam said.

The Kijkaan shook his head incredulously. "I've heard of squatters, but I was always under the impression people wanted squatters to *leave*, not rally around them."

No response.

He laughed. "I feel like I'm as mystified by the idea of a movement as you are of my ignorance."

"They made a musical about it," Alex said.

He shook his head. "I don't do much theatre. Where is she based? Loisaida, I mean."

"It's in the name. She's on the Lower East Side."

He rubbed his chin. "Now that I think about it, I do remember hearing about homeless riots in the news around that time. Was the representative part of that?"

Sam sighed, retrieved her bag from between her feet, slung it over her shoulder, and joined Nails outside the door.

"Oh, I'm sorry, I didn't mean to offend you."

She waved him away.

"We want to go!" Nails shouted.

The Kijkaan raised his hands in surrender. "All right, all right. I shouldn't hold you. I'll open the door at the top of the stairs."

"Will you actually, though, or is there some kind of catch before we can get home?" Nails demanded.

"The only catch is you'll still have to get home."

"We'll deal," Nails said. "Let's get the fuck out."

The lights in the hallway were stingingly bright, and the bitter smell of mold was braced with the sweet smell of roach shit. The walls felt slick and tacky when Alex touched them. Nails led the way, pushing open the stairwell door and bolting up the steps. There was a hole in the brick ceiling above them, big enough for them to crawl through. Nails pulled himself up first. His boots disappeared through the hole as Alex followed.

The darkness around them was so complete. Alex blinked to see if his eyes were closed. He tripped over Nails on the landing. Sam's flashlight stretched across the floor as she grabbed the lip of the entrance and pulled herself up, lighting up the room enough to show an old, broken storage room. The fake drywall ceiling had exploded into confetti years before, and what was once stacks of cardboard boxes had collapsed into thick, papery mush. Nails sat back, winced, pushed a brick out from under him, and sat again.

"I'm thirsty," he complained.

"Yeah," Sam said as she scanned the room for a door. She put down the flashlight and grabbed a stack of boxes, but before she could move them, the whole stack disintegrated into a white cloud of grit and flakes.

"Are you OK?" Alex called.

He was answered by a series of sneezes. She kicked her way out of the pile of rotten cardboard to grab the flashlight off the floor and pointed it back through the thinning cloud, but there was nothing but another wall behind it.

"Where is this damn door?" she demanded.

A bright square of light appeared in the dark and cast a halo around Nails's face. "Listen, I've got a signal, so worst comes to worst, we can call somebody to come get us."

Alex's eye caught a dark shadow against one wall and pointed Sam's flashlight directly at it. There was the doorway standing behind a pile of boxes and broken canvas pushcarts. Nails whooped and jumped off the floor. They piled through the doorway, over planks of wood crossed on top of the broken floor, and down a tight brick hallway full of more ripped and fraying canvas carts. At the end of the hallway was a thin plaster wall. Before they could agree on punching through it, they discovered it was just leaning against a wooden frame. They pushed it aside and walked into another large storage room, carefully organized, stamped everywhere with the Home Depot logo, and lit with glowing computer screens. They weaved through the computer desks straight for the exit sign.

"What about the alarm?" Alex asked once they'd reached the door.

Sam shrugged and pushed it open. The siren wailed all around them.

"What a *fucking* asshole!" Nails cried, shoving them through the door. They jumped down from the loading dock and forced open the gate enough to squeeze through. The street on the other side was mostly empty except for one old homeless man who stared at them as they ran out the back door. They got around the corner and off the block before anyone could catch up with them, and once they were far enough away not to hear the siren blare, they slowed down. They dusted themselves off and helped each other slap clean hard-to-reach spots.

Alex realized with a tremor that the sun was gone. The late-night traffic was slow on the avenue; cars breezed by calmly, a handful of drunk people were yelling at each other as they stumbled away from a bar, workers on the graveyard shift chatted on the corner, and a group of girls was howling up at the night sky, triumphant of their total domination of the night. The broad boulevard was practically empty, and the usual busy humming was dulled; it was a quiet Thursday morning.

They found the 181st street station with no problem, and, after an hour, the train pulled into the station, shuddering and squealing through every rotation of wheels. It dragged itself into its setting and collapsed.

Nails fell asleep against Alex's shoulder, jostling lightly with the train's rocking. Meanwhile, Alex and Sam checked the business card. It was a plain white business card, without any strange markings, or textures. There was a phone number, and an address, and one word at the top.

Kijkaan
Sub-basement

Sam nodded silently, folded the card back into her pocket, and chuckled.

"You guys should stay at my place tonight. Trains to Brooklyn are gonna take forever," she said.

Alex bounced Nails's cheek against his shoulder until his eyes opened a crack. "Sam asked if you want to stay at her place tonight."

Nails shrugged, rolled over, and fell asleep against the hand rest.

Alex let his eyes close lulled by the warm train. He felt Nails start awake and slump back to sleep when the train kicked forward and heard the tinny sound of muffled music from Sam's headphones.

Chapter Five

ALEX DREAMED HE was back in the Kijkaan's basement. The Kijkaan's eyes shined like flares in a darkness so thick with mold he could feel the spores on his skin.

"You left too soon," he said. "I feel terrible about our meeting. I wanted to make it up to you."

Alex could barely focus on his words. He was exhausted. He tried to roll away from him, but the Kijkaan stopped him and rolled him back.

"Perhaps I can do something for the Lord," the Kijkaan continued. "What does she ask for in fealty? Who falls under her protection? Does she have authority outside New York?"

Too blearly to think, instinct told Alex it was better to say nothing.

The Kijkaan watched him and waited. When no answer came, he changed the topic. "How many people did Sam travel with? Do you remember when she went missing and when she came back?"

Alex's mind skipped over the few details Sam gave him. "Didn't you already say you weren't helping us?" he asked.

The Kijkaan's eyes glowed. "I've changed my mind."

There was an odd quality to his voice, like a record with the speed adjusted. His words seem to land with more weight, and yet the whispered quality made them sound fuzzy. "Find Sam's friends, then."

"You still don't have the information I need to do that," he reminded Alex gently. Alex shrugged. If the Kijkaan couldn't do the one thing they needed from him, then he couldn't help. He tried to drift back to sleep, but the Kijkaan nudged him awake. *"But there are other things that I can do. What do you need?"*

Alex tried again to ignore him. He was annoyed but so, so tired. Why wouldn't the Kijkaan leave him alone? And how did he get there, Alex wondered with a little more alarm. He'd have to ask Nails in the morning.

The Kijkaan nudged him again. "What do you need?"

"A job," Alex snapped angrily.

"I can get you a job," the Kijkaan replied quickly. "Just tell me why you were in the Tunnels."

"For Sam," Alex said, grabbing his pillow and covering his face.

"What about the Lord?" the Kijkaan asked, pawing at his shoulder. Alex shrugged him off angrily. "Your Lady? Loisaida? Why did she send you?"

"Leave me alone."

"What does she want in Thundertown?"

He threw aside his pillow and rolled over.

"I don't know!" he shouted.

He woke up suddenly on the floor of Sam's living room, submerged in the nest of their coats. The room was flooded with the copper light of late afternoon, and Nails was in the kitchen helping himself to the fridge. Alex's mind was alert inside the heavy shell of his body, his blood still surging from the shock of his dream.

Nails noticed him moving and spoke through a mouthful of food. "What'd you tell him?"

"Who?" Alex asked instantly. Nails cocked his head and gave him a look, silently asking if he really needed that answered. "...you saw the Kijkaan, too?"

Nails rolled his eyes incredulously. "Yeah."

"He asked me about the senator and Sam. There was nothing to say."

Nails scooped cereal out of the bowl in his hand and rambled over to sit on the couch, his long legs twining like rubber. "I was thinking we should ask Loisaida about him and why people are going missing."

There were unspoken accusations in that statement. Alex pushed himself up and lurched towards the counter. "Let me have some coffee before we start talking about this."

They looked through the cabinets for coffee. They found the filter with the mugs, and finally, the coffee in the freezer. After a light search for the kettle, they filled a pot with hot water and waited for it to boil on the stove. Once it reached a simmer, they figured they'd waited long enough and poured hot water down the filter.

Alex replayed the dream in his mind; however, awake, the only details that stayed were the Kijkaan's burning eyes and mold. He wondered if the venue for their conversation was his skull, or the Kijkaan's. Was it more like two voices on the phone or players in a theatre? The telepathic conversations he saw on TV didn't prepare him for the existential confusion of wondering whose words were whose.

"Did Battle Row ever do the dream thing?"

Nails shook his head. "I never had that done to me before."

"It felt weird."

Sam came into the living room, found a chair, and sat down with the palm of her hand still grinding into her eye.

"Did you hear from the Kijkaan?" Nails asked.

"He asked me about Loisaida and what I did in Thundertown," she said, scrubbing the fuzz on her head. "What's he want from us?"

"He's an information broker. What else does he want?" Nails asked.

"Why wouldn't he want money?" Alex asked. "When we asked how we could pay him, he said he wanted money."

"Dude never even heard about the Tompkins Square riots. Obviously, he wants to expand," Nails said.

That only made Alex wonder why those plans weren't already in place when he made steps to build an entire underground city.

"I told Alex I wanted to go talk to Loisaida again," Nails said, as the other two ate. "I want to ask her why people are going missing."

Sam shot a glance at Alex. "What if she doesn't know?"

"Why wouldn't she? She's a Lord, right? She goes to the courts, and she hears about it."

After five, Alex called Loisaida. Her voice was clipped and her questions short, but she kept the conversation up even when it was obvious she wanted to hang up.

"So you found a Thundertown after all? I'm glad you all came back all right. Does Sam still want to talk?"

"Yeah. Thanks."

"No problem. What about the police? Have you heard back from them?"

"Not yet. When we were up there, we met this guy with a whole collection of missing persons files. It made me want to ask you if you knew how many people were missing."

Her silence said she didn't. "A what?"

"He had a lot of files on missing people," Alex said again.

"What was he doing with them?"

"Hiring people to find them and bring them back to him."

"Find who? Where?"

"Missing people. Underground."

Loisaida lapsed into another tense silence. "Listen...I can't talk now. Let me call you back."

"OK."

"Anywhere before nine in the morning, is that all right?"

"Sure."

WHEN THEY REACHED the Gross House, he looked over the damage the Tunnels had done to his clothes. His pants would need patching, both sleeves of his coat were torn in different places, a rotten seam on his vest had finally burst, and everything needed to be washed. He tossed the pants aside and began mending. When his eyes were too strained to keep sewing and his hand was starting to go numb, he made a few last stitches to close the hole. Then he took a break to boil water and washed everything in the tub.

Hours passed without a call from Loisaida.

The fridge was empty when Alex checked it, and the last of his coffee was gone. Nails was on his laptop at the kitchen table. It was harder to share a room with him now than it was in high school. Nails's bedroom in his childhood home near mid-town was smaller and had a lot more stuff, but it felt more cramped in the Gross House. Maybe it was because Alex was actually living there and not spending the night four days out of the week.

He had to dig through Nails's stuff to get to his clothes. Nails left food in their room. Alex's bed was crammed in one corner and was a foot and a half away from Nail's cot, but at least he wasn't sleeping on the floor anymore. They had to negotiate time alone, and now that he didn't have any privacy, it was all he wanted. He needed space, but in order to have space, he needed money. For money, he needed a job, and wondering why he didn't have one made him miserable.

He wondered if the change came from Nails losing the place he'd lived in his whole life. He and his mother were comfortable there, even if they were a little boxed in. He couldn't imagine what it was like to be stable one day and not the next.

Alex's mom didn't believe in Lords. According to his grandparents, the family lost their faith in the court system during the Second World War. His mom said they lost it hundreds of years ago during colonialism. Their different politics was what made holidays hard.

"Did you and Mama Kaczorowski need to pay fealty?" he asked.

Nails snorted. "Oh, yeah."

"Really?"

"Hell's kitchen was bad, my dude."

Alex snorted. "Oh, please."

"OK. First of all, it still wasn't great when I was growing up, but that's beside the point. My point is, it's still right off Times Square, and there's been a power vacuum there since the Astors abdicated in '98. It's the most expensive slice of tourist real estate in the country. If anybody says they're Boss, twenty people jump them. Sometimes a whole bunch of them say they're the New Astor and start brawling in the street, and some of them even go after the Broadway Mayor for his territory. We couldn't only have a house block."

"When was this happening when I was over there?"

"You were there when they caved in 10th Ave."

Thinking back, he did remember getting dragged off the couch early in the morning to look at an enormous hole under the expressway, and people in the crowd around them were excitedly telling the story of what happened by flapping their arms and making explosion sounds. At the time, it registered as one of those strange little moments in life that fades under the weight of bigger ones.

"And what about that time my building caught on fire?" Nails added. The look on Alex's face made him throw his arms out. "How do you not remember that? We went to the store, picked up some beers, and started walking back as the firefighters were hosing down the building!"

"I remember that, but you didn't tell me what it was about."

"We were both there when my mom said it got started by a *flying disembodied head*."

"And that has what to do with Times Square?"

"Because!" Nails cried. He rubbed his eyes. "Fine, fine. So maybe you couldn't've guessed from that, but I figured you did."

"Why?"

"Because you're a living person with eyes and ears that work?"

Alex scoffed.

"That's not a crazy thought to have. It's in the news, like, all the time."

He felt it was time to change the subject. "Anyways, I asked because I wanted to know what Battle Row did."

"You didn't get the best impression from him. He's touchy—maybe a little sensitive—but Battle Row's the guy you want in a fight. He doesn't do theatrics, and he finished a fight without flooding the whole neighborhood. Speaking of you not reading the news, I found this."

He beckoned Alex over and turned the laptop to face him. On the screen was a news article commenting on record numbers of disappearances in four of the five boroughs. Staten Island was untouched, but community leaders in Queens, Brooklyn, Manhattan, the Bronx, and even parts of Long Island were all reporting escalating numbers of missing persons reports.

Meanwhile, trasgo in Thundertown were complaining about packs of humans wandering through their territories, and the NYPD responded with a passive-aggressive press statement saying that none of this would be happening if abandoned structures stayed empty. The statement went on to say that, of course, affected families would get as much help as they needed, provided that didn't violate the delicate trust of the Alvar Courts. Both Day and Night Courts had equally withering official statements saying that they would love to work with the police if the police stopped evicting people below ground through no-knock raids. The Mayor's office, likewise, had an official statement blaming State regulations for their lack of action, and the State declined to write an official quote.

It felt so safe and distant in the article with facts checked and players identified. He was so removed he had the luxury of being no more affected than a little annoyed that it was happening.

He glanced at the date on the article. "Me, not reading the news? Why couldn't you find this article back when Sam was missing?"

"'Cause I'm a fuck up, too. What do you want from me? Anyways, I e-mailed it to Sam. I don't know what to do with this information, but I figured she'd want it anyways."

If the articles were over a month old, then the problem predated Sam's missing persons case. "Did you find any more articles about this?"

"Some local news about the people that are missing."

"Nothing from outside the City?"

"Nope."

"It didn't go national?" he asked with a touch of surprise.

Nails shrugged.

Alex chewed on a lock of hair thoughtfully. "Sam said she went missing while on the subway. Did you see anything from the MTA?"

He waved his hand. "I'll check. Go get food. I'm starving."

ALEX PASSED TWO men slapping paperwork at each other on the floor outside the factory. He stepped quietly over Joe, who was still asleep in the stairwell despite the noise. It was cold in the street, and the cloud cover was so dark and heavy, it looked as if the rooftops were holding it up. The warehouse across the street had a few trucks in the loading dock, and the door was up on the garage across the street. An old Chinese man rolled idly across the empty dock in an office chair waiting.

Alex turned the corner into the neighborhood of three-family houses, the occasional five-story apartment building, and truck lots. It was a quiet neighborhood with few cars, but he could see the highway a few blocks north at every intersection. He entered the bodega and ordered two cold sandwiches and two bags of chips.

Back at the apartment, one of the workers stood in the factory doorway, fanning himself with his cap. He stared at Alex and gave him a half-hearted whistle as he passed. Alex wondered if the man thought he was a woman.

Nails had moved to their room and changed his clothes and was still on the computer chewing hard on his left thumb. He did a double-take when Alex entered the room and pushed the laptop towards him.

"Found this for you. What'd you order?" he asked, jumping on the bag of sandwiches.

"Buffalo turkey, queso blanco, and some barbecue chips."

"Shweet." He broke open the bag of chips first, while Alex looked at the screen. Nails was past missing persons cases and onto stories about a recent MTA worker's strike.

According to the articles, walkouts were happening all over the City, although the MTA wasn't recognizing it as an official strike.

Their employees had a long list of complaints; blackouts, earthquakes, unexplained dizziness, equipment failure, missing equipment, broken locks in employee spaces, unauthorized entry into employee spaces, radio mishandling, unannounced schedule changes, and poor ventilation. The phenomenons seemed like a haunted house with workers describing the lights flickering, figures appearing in the dark, lockers broken into, and property destroyed. Equipment as small as a radio or as big as the entire information booth at the station entrance vanished without warning.

A worker at the Times Square Station described unlocking an employee bathroom to find themselves instead in a snowy courtyard. There was no official statement as of yet. Station management gave excuses for the lost equipment, broken furniture, the flickering lights, the shapes they saw, and the things they heard but still suggested that these were all the symptoms of an undiagnosed issue.

Alex looked up to find Nails layering chips inside his sandwich.

"Did Miss Lower East Side ever call you back last night?" Nails asked.

Alex reached for his sandwich. "Not yet."

"What's taking so long?" he muttered sourly.

LOISAIDA HELD HER face in her hands. There was too much work to think about the call from Alex, but working in the office alone shattered her discipline. All it took was one phone call to clear her brain of everything but the heavy implication that there was some person out there collecting people's information—or so this person told a little group of kids that wandered into his territory asking very specific questions. God knew what kind of conclusions he drew from seeing them, but it clearly made him feel important enough to run his scam on the kids, and now that he had her name, he'd run it on her, too.

There were full names buried in some half-forgotten basement somewhere in Harlem. Someone collected information on the missing to prey on the frightened.

She put one hand down and felt around the desk for her phone and found it behind a bottle of water, a book, and three photocopied Parks Department complaints. She opened her contacts list, typed in a name, and put the phone to her ear.

Chief Tal of the Ninth Precinct answered the phone. After exchanging pleasantries, Loisaida got down to business. "I was wondering if the NYPD hired an information broker from uptown, somewhere near the old Thunder Tunnels."

"The Thunder Tunnels are a long ways away from One Police Plaza," Tal pointed out with a thick clearing of his throat. "It's not likely I'd hear anything from the Heights, but I can give you a number to call."

She pressed her lips together. "Can you do me a favor?"

A nervous chuckle. "Thought that's what I was doing."

"I need this to be a department-wide request. You need to make the call," she said.

There was a pause. Loisaida held her breath. As one of the few Lords with a solid grasp on modern law, she provided a lifeline between the courts and the state. Asking a police chief to make calls for her like her secretary was pushing the limit of her privileges.

When he responded, his voice was low. "How am I supposed to explain that to people?"

Loisaida took a deep breath. This needed to be done carefully; if she was too casual, he wouldn't take it seriously. Too serious, and she'd scare him off. "Explain? What do you need to explain? You're the one looking for the explanation. If anybody asks questions, tell them one of your local Lords asked why someone all the way in the Heights had information on her people."

"This is too much," Tal said. "That's crossing a line. I don't want to make anybody think I'm getting between some of youses. They might call me up to deal with one of your fights."

"Tal--"

"I'm just a guy," he pressed. "I'm nothing special, got no talents, just a badge and a job. If they start putting me between some of youse guys and I get hit by a bolt of lightning, I'm gonna get smoked."

Loisaida exhaled. It wasn't a yes, but at least he didn't seem offended. She pressed on. "I agree, but the NYPD's formal, diplomatic distance from the courts results in a gulf between members of our respective institutions, don't you think? It disappoints me that so many go without police protection because of it."

Silence. She worried about laying the bullshit on a little thick, but Tal responded well. "Between you and me, I totally agree. Putting out a bulletin about trasgo informants would be a lot easier for me than it would be for you. But you know how it is. I don't call the shots."

"I know," she soothed. Then, thinking he'd like the narrative of a martyr, added, "Doing the right thing is hell. And nobody thanks you for it."

"I hear you."

"You're a good man, Tal."

He was chuckling as she hung up. She went back to rubbing her temples. It would be much more complicated to find out if this person was being paid by a Lord; first, she'd have to post the question in the Night Court, the Day Court, and then to each of the breakaway Unions formed throughout New York and New Jersey. If nothing came to light, she'd have to find some way to round up the Petty Lords. It would be hard, tedious work, and she had a feeling it would leave her unrewarded.

Her instincts said this person was acting alone for their own benefit. Rarely did scams survive a conspiracy, when scam artists were notoriously hard to work with. In the brief conversation she had with Alex, she'd formed a complete image of this person as a freelance agent, who was fishing for rewards by offering up lost constituents to Lords for a modest price. By doing the work for them, they could take a cut, and the Lord could pretend they did the work themselves. Of course, the problem with her theory was that this Person was introducing himself to every human he found, which undermined the Lords' reputations. Was he performing charity as some form of challenge? If he was, how did he think he'd survive that campaign?

She was getting lost in questions she couldn't answer. She'd heard about the disappearances, but what she heard hadn't lead her to believe this was an epidemic. The police knew to pass cases along to the courts when they fell under their jurisdiction, and when someone's loved one approached their local Lord to act on their behalf, that was business as usual.

Finding Sam was easy; she asked one intern to put up fliers and another to give more to allies underground. She suspected her peers in the courts didn't talk about the case because they didn't see it as a big deal either, but now somebody was filling a need she didn't know was lacking. No answers were coming out of the walls. She turned her phone over and called up Alex's number.

ALEX'S PHONE RANG. He wiped chip crumbs on his pants and answered the call.

"Alex? It's Senator Loisaida. I called to talk about the person you met yesterday."

"I figured."

"Did he tell you anything else about himself?"

"Nope. He's an information broker. He talks like he's been in the neighborhood a while, and he's got a bunch of filing cabinets. He calls himself the Kijkaan. That's it."

"Don't—!" she started, but cut herself off.

He froze. Silence stretched on the other side of the phone. "Don't what?"

Loisaida sighed. "You don't have much experience with the Folk do you?"

"I do," he argued.

"You don't act like it. Be careful with names, they're powerful, and people can use them against you," she warned. "What did he ask from you?"

"He wanted us to get him in contact with you."

"That doesn't surprise me."

He tried to bring the conversation back to the point. "Is anybody from your territory in any of those files?"

"You were the first person to approach me with a missing persons case."

"Then you don't know what's going on?"

"No."

"How could you not—" He cut himself off and started again, from a friendlier angle. "Sam still wants to go down there and find her friends, but we don't know what 'there' is."

"It's an extension of the City," she soothed. "Just as old and busy."

"That doesn't help. How are we supposed to find them? Why are they even there? Why can't anyone tell us what's going on?"

She didn't answer immediately. Anxiety crept into his belly and up his spine as he wondered whether he should have expected to be told anything. Battle Row snapped at them for less; he should have been grateful the senator returned any of their calls.

To his surprise, she sighed. "I'm sorry; I *should* have answers. I promise you that I'll have some for you and the people under my protection by the end of the month."

He'd never heard a Lord apologize before. "Thanks."

"No. Thank you," she said.

Alex hung up, feeling no less confused than before.

"What'd she say?" Nails asked from across the table, his eyes narrow with suspicion.

Alex looked up from his phone. "She says she doesn't know anything about this."

He rolled his eyes. "Bullshit."

Alex thought again about meeting the King of Battle Row, and how Nails stepped away when he turned to face them. "What makes you say that?"

"Because it doesn't make sense." Nails snapped, wringing his hands.

"Why not? Why can't she not know?"

Nails swung his hands around and clapped them on his head. "She's a Lord, dude. What'd she do to make you so loyal to her?"

"She apologized to me, for one."

Nails snorted. "*You're* easy,"

Chapter Six

NAILS WAS ON his laptop in the common space in the same pants and shirt from three days earlier. His eyes shuttered in the way that forewarned he was on the verge of collapse.

"Go to sleep," Alex suggested.

Nails gave him a look that said he wished it was that easy.

"Can I borrow that to apply to a couple more jobs?" he added.

Nails looked at his computer, then at Alex. "Do you wanna, like, do something?"

Alex paused, confused. "What? No. I mean, why?"

"I was thinking about how long we've been in this room for."

"You don't need to go out, dude. You need to sleep. And I'm broke."

"I could cover for you if you wanted me to."

"You need to sleep," Alex repeated. There was nothing he wanted more than to get out of Cieri house, breathe fresh air, and see good friends. Company would balance his mind. But if he wanted to see people, he would need to buy a Metrocard.

"Nothing really happening tonight except for post-punk night at the Glacier, but it's seven bucks for a DJ."

"So let's not do that."

"I guess that's what you expect on a Tuesday night," Nails muttered. "Do we know anybody around here?"

"Yeah, but not really." The neighborhood was filled with people they knew, but only through two or three degrees of separation. If they showed up to their door with friends, they'd be warmly received, but alone they would be trespassing.

"We could always go over to the Card House."

There was the same problem there as visiting any of the houses in Brooklyn. Alex kneaded the heel of his hand into his eye as a tension headache started to crest. "Who's over there?"

"You don't know?"

"There's Erica Kettle, Donnie, Magi and his girlfriend—"

Nails perked up. "Wait...*Magi*? Since when? I been wondering where he was! What's the story with this girl?"

Alex shrugged. "I don't know her."

Nails raised his eyebrow. He always raised the right one, with a small bald scar in the ridge. "How'd you hear about her?"

Alex shrugged. "From Magi, where else?"

"Since when do you talk to him?"

He frowned. "Why not?"

Nails waved his hand to strike his question from the record. "You said you never met this girl before. That's enough for me. Let's call him and head out."

"Dude, no. You need to sleep."

"Yeah, but I'm not tired right now, so if we go out, then I can get tired," Nails said.

"But--" Alex began, about to plead the case for his body and mind to get the rest they needed to keep him healthy and happy.

Nails cut him off by bouncing out of his seat and into the room to grab his coat and shoes. "C'mon, I'll buy you some beer."

THE CARD HOUSE was one of the old squats in the Lower East Side with a long, checkerboard history. Anytime Alex spent more than an hour there, he could rely on one of the older residents to wander and over drunkenly recite its history. It was built in 1910 as a tenement. In the twenties, a tailor was built on the ground floor, quickly expanding to the whole building. By 1932, there was a storefront on the ground floor, workshops on the second and third, and storage on the fourth. By the forties, the third floor was a call center and a garage around the corner was drafted as a small truck depot. In the fifties, local demand for warehouse deals on fabric slowed, and bigger businesses outbid them on interstate deals. The tailor closed after over fifty years of business, and the grandson of the shop's founder moved to Long Island. He tried once or twice to lease apartments in the building, then put it on the market.

An award-winning picture was taken in the building's doorway in 1976 when a man passed out in a pile of bricks.

In the mid-nineties, squatters applied for tenant's protection. They cleared crumbling plaster, repainted the walls, anchored wobbly stairs, and tried without success to establish an official relationship with the gas and power companies, but they defaulted instead to siphoning them from any outlet they could find. The name 'Card House' came from a comment about the support beams.

The tailor's grandson died in 2009 of kidney failure, and in 2012, after a twenty-year struggle, the last remaining group of core tenants was awarded the building.

Before long, they arrived. Alex knocked on the door. Magi answered, barefoot but layered in shirts: a promotional T-shirt, an open button-up, a flannel, a cardigan, and another, heavier sweater on top of that.

Magi was a black kid with uncombed, natural hair, who was always blinking at the world through dirty glasses and a slightly confused expression. For the past four months, he'd been ducking his parents. They wanted him to get a STEM degree, but all he wanted to pursue a degree in Aetheric Design.

"How long you been living here?" Nails asked.

"Oh, I'm not. My friend Mika's been letting me stay for—"

Nails didn't let him finish. "About her...who's she? How come I never heard of her before?"

He looked between them helplessly. "It's not like that."

"No, she just lets you stay at her house for however long."

"Not too long," Magi said quietly, staring down at his toes.

Nails grinned. "Just until the war between you and your parents ends?"

"It will."

Alex was surprised, and judging by the look on his face, Nails was too. Boosting Magi over fences and finding places out of sight to hide him had become a reliable way to energize a boring night.

"We've been talking," he explained. "They think I should take a rest year."

"A rest year? Merlin didn't take a rest year, and neither will the secrets of the universe," Nails declared. When Magi didn't laugh, he quickly changed the subject. "Tell me about this girl. Does she pray to shapes, too?"

He blinked. "Does she what?"

"Pray to shapes. Like that sacred geometry you're always talking about."

"Oh," Magi said, frowning deeper. "Sacred geometry is based on real mathematical formulas that were used around the world for thousands of years to build buildings and study the stars. It's not a belief system. It's math."

"Oh," Nails imitated. "*Oh.*"

Magi wilted.

A door slammed on the floor above him, and an older white woman in a sweatsuit nailed them with a nasty look. "Sheldon!"

Alex and Nails both looked at Magi, named Sheldon by his parents. His shoulders climbed up slowly to meet his ears.

"Bonnie," he answered.

"Who's that?" She snapped, pointing at Nails and Alex.

Magi snuck them a glance out of the corner of his eye. "Friends."

"You've been inviting a lot of people over lately, and I don't think I've seen any of them twice! Do you think that's respectful? In fact, have you thought about anyone else in this building since you moved in?" She pounded her fist on the banister before he could answer. "You're in a collective living situation, which means you need to take responsibility for the consequences of your actions. You can invite all the 'friends' you want—you can invite the whole damn city, for all I care—but you're the one who's gonna be dealing with the cops when they come."

"Cops?" he repeated.

"Yes, the cops! Your parents are looking for you, haven't you noticed the cops? They're all around the building! There was one sitting in his car right out in front! He was there for hours until I knocked on the window and asked for his badge number. He tried to hide it from me, but he was in a no-parking zone idling all morning. And nobody noticed!" Bonnie shouted, slamming her fist again on the banister.

Magi's confused expression only got more pinched. "But my parents know where I am."

A door above them burst open and a voice shouted, "*Shut the fuck up!*"

"We're going to talk about this later, Sheldon," she shouted, as she scurried back to her apartment. "We'll see how big you feel without your friends behind you."

"I don't feel—" Magi began, but she was already gone. He lowered his head and led the way to the apartment, which was small, cold, and filled with overflowing black milk crates. There was a young woman wearing lots of baggy fabric, who looked up and around with a bored, slow blink, unimpressed by everything.

"Mika, this is Nails and Alex," Magi said.

Alex began to shuck his coat, but the cold made him pull it back up. "Is the heat off?"

Mika rolled her eyes. "The boiler doesn't work. They bought one in the nineties to replace the original temporarily. It was never meant to heat all three floors."

"How much is a new one?"

"Not that much, but since this whole place is falling apart, it's tough to agree on what the bigger priorities are."

"I think I could fix it," Magi said.

"Do you know anything about boilers?" Alex asked.

"No, but I can find a design for that model."

Alex had a series of vivid flashbacks to every news headline he'd ever seen about an Aether enthusiast accidentally blowing themselves up. "Maybe you should buy a new boiler."

"We will, but maybe I can fix it now." He got up and went to one of the stacks of milk crates. "Here, look. I'll show you what I mean."

"Don't," he begged, but it was too late. Magi had his laptop open and was doing research.

Nails, meanwhile, turned to Mika. "So, how'd you two meet?"

"We're not dating," Magi and Mika said at once.

Nails jolted, surprised by their combined denial. "I didn't say you were. I was just curious about how you met."

Magi rubbed his nose. "Um...here."

Nails waited. He fidgeted more. "I was hanging out in the park all summer and spent some nights here. We started talking."

Mika had a clearer timeline of events. "There was an art performance on the roof. I wasn't gonna go, but I went to check it out, and he made it fun."

"Aw," Alex said.

She rolled her eyes.

"How'd you end up in the house?"

"You know Squalor? He's my uncle. He's one of the original people who opened the squat up, but he found a better deal in Maryland. Most of this stuff is still his."

She gestured around the room, to the folding table, the chairs around it, the dishes boxes stacked in the corner.

A few minutes later, Magi announced he had a design that might fix the boiler.

"I don't want to be here for this," Alex said.

"No, no, no, I just need to look at it to make sure I have the right design. I won't do anything. I'm just going to look at it." He tucked his laptop under his arm and lead them down into the basement, where he compared the boiler to the diagrams on his screen.

"All right. Well, this is for a newer style of boiler, but all the same valves and stuff are there, so I think this could work. I'm going to try to see if I can balance it out. I think that'll make it start again."

"No!" Alex cried.

"No, listen. It's OK. I'm just tricking the boiler into acting like it's getting started—"

"That's a bad idea. Those are the designs that act like turning off all the safety features."

"That's not true," Magi argued. He put his laptop down and got out a piece of chalk. "Don't worry. This is easy,"

"Dude—" Alex took a step forward to stop him, but Mika put her arm out.

"Relax, he's got this."

"He does not!"

Magi was done before they could argue and smiled proudly when all the arrows on the boiler jumped back to green. They went upstairs expecting the room to warm up, but an hour later, it was still cold as a stone. Magi went back downstairs to check on the boiler and came up looking embarrassed.

"I think I changed the meter and not the pressure," he said sadly.

Everything got a little blurry after a few beers. Alex lay perfectly still on the couch, breathing slowly to stem nausea and watched the ceiling spin. The couch felt funny, like it was old enough to push the frame through the cushions. He closed his eyes and felt waves of nausea lap over him. He'd feel better if he puked, but puking was a disgusting, painful process. He tried to think of some other way to relieve the tension in his belly, like drinking water, but when he opened his eyes, the dizziness nailed him to the couch. Better to lay back and wait, he decided. The others sounded like they were having a lot more fun far away on the other side of the apartment. After an eternity lying paralyzed on the mattress, Nails came to check on him.

"Wanna sit up?"

"Nah."

"Want some water?"

"Could you?"

He made an effort to sit up as Nails handed him the glass of water. His head immediately began to spin, but he forced himself to choke down a mouthful, which tasted lukewarm and stale after the beer.

Alex waited for the spinning to slow down, wondering what was Squalor's and what was Mika's. The curtains were nailed to the wall, and the cupboards were plain, square boxes warped with wear. He noticed that the couch wasn't a couch, but milk crates stuffed full of pillows and covered with a blanket.

He was thinking, but he was too drunk to make it make sense. A connection was forming between the Card House squatters and himself—they might have solutions to problems he had at home. He should ask them about it. What did he want to ask them? He took another sip.

Alex was thinking about something. He was thinking about the stories the squatters told about fixing things themselves. Back when things were wild, and the Lower East Side empty, a lot of Rogue Folk came out of the river and the gutters looking for a better place to stay.

"Hey, Magi," Alex said. "Or Mika. Do you know how everybody here got their protection?"

"What protection?"

"The...for the...protection from...everything. Aether protection," he struggled to arrange his thoughts, then switched the statement to a question. "You guys don't pay fealty, right?"

"Oh...no. We've got a bunch of wards. Protection blocks."

"That's enough?" Nails asked.

"Spray a little Raid or bury some mothballs to keep the small stuff out," Mika added.

"What if you got Rogue Folk bigger than your average butterfly? What if they're big enough to eat your food and use your toilet?"

"You get a lawyer," Mika said.

"Seriously?"

She shrugged. "Or get your dead."

"You guys got dead here?" Alex asked.

"You know some of them," Mika said, counting the names off in her fingers. "Little John, Countess, Chechen Jim. Sarah says her husband is possessing her radio, so she won't let us use him."

"Is he?" Alex asked.

She shrugged.

"Imagine if they did that to you," he muttered, overwhelmed by dizziness and the existential horror of being a defense block for the rest of eternity.

"I wouldn't notice. You don't pull a soul out of Heaven to build a shield," Magi muttered.

"Lies," Nails said. "A Jewish conspiracy. I choose to believe the government is hiding their direct D.C.-to-Heaven pipeline from the American people."

"You can have that fantasy," Magi said. "You're welcome to believe whatever you want, so long as you're not trying to stop anyone else because you think Aetheric Engineering interferes with God's plan, somehow."

"I do," Nails agreed. "And I will."

"Or that the whole practice has been run by the Devil himself since the beginning of time."

"He is. Saw it on YouTube."

"And then try to prove it by bringing in different religious symbols from all around the world and pretending that they mean the same things."

"Are we talking about the same video? Can we watch it?" Nails asked.

"How can you prove they can't think?" Alex asked sluggishly.

Magi furiously counted off reasons on his hands. "They don't react to outside stimuli. They don't recognize things. They don't recognize people. They can't perform any basic actions to prove they're intelligent. There are studies going back for centuries, trying and failing to determine sentience in constructs. You could read for the rest of your life and not find a positive result."

"That's not what my extensive YouTube and Wikipedia research tells me," Nails said.

Alex felt an odd mix of lethargy and energy. "My house as a kid was haunted."

"Stable Aether constructs aren't ghosts," Magi insisted, practically spitting with fury. "This is like really for real believing dolls have souls because they've got two arms and two legs. Aether constructs can take any shape the designer wants, and sometimes they choose deceased family members. And you know why? Because it's easy. You've got everything you need to fill out the formula; mass, volume, shape. Program basic actions for it to perform and give it a name to answer to. Easier to do it with something that already existed then to build your whole own thing. But even if they *were* ghosts, then that would prove they're not smart, because all they do is repeat the same thing over and over! Ghosts have no substance. Ghosts are like...recordings and sometimes they get distorted. Back in my grandpa's town, there's a story of a kid who drowned at the beach, who always appears during tourist season and scares the shit out of the lifeguards. My grandpa told me one day he grew to be twenty feet tall, still drowning. The hotel called an engineer to fix him, and she traced the problem back to a cast put down by a scuba diving company to make the coral around their property look bigger."

"So?" Alex asked.

"So, he's not alive; he's from another time. He's out there in the water at the same time every day for the entire spring, but his body's not there anymore. His parents took him home and buried him. If he was smart, why wouldn't he get out? Or sink to the bottom and walk away? Why doesn't he know he's buried? The parts they use in blocks aren't metaphysical; they're *facts*. They're weight, height, age, and names. Parameters. Description. Designs need variables, not souls."

"So, basically witchcraft," Nails said.

"No!" Magi shouted.

Alex walked into Mika's bathroom and poured out the contents of his stomach. Afterward, he felt much better.

ALEX LIVED IN Stuyvesant Town back when it was still Section 8 housing. His mother worked less than ten minutes away, at St. Vincent's, but they had to move when she made the change from medical staff to administration.

Their next home was uptown on the Eastside. He remembered hating everything about the building, from the boring grey bricks outside to the windows looking out onto an air shaft. There were only a few kids his age in the neighborhood, and they were too wrapped up in their own business to get the new kid up to speed. Fortunately, they moved out a year later.

He spent most of that year in the park down the street, hiding from the other kids and looking for something to do. There was a community garden near the park run mostly by old people, who gave him tasks and told him stories. He found cats in the garden, but unlike any other cat that came into his life, he was forbidden to touch them. He tried to pet one in secret and got mauled by two others hiding in the bushes waiting for him to lean forward enough to be off-balance. He ran screaming back to his mother, who picked him up and carried him all the way downtown for a tetanus shot.

In the winter, when the park was bare, the cats hid all over the block. They popped up inside the building from the roof to the basement, to the airshaft under Alex's window. He could hear them howling at night, high-pitched, mournful and terrifyingly human.

During the day, when he could see them in the airshaft, he knew they were cats. At night, when logic ebbed away, the sound haunted him. Their wailing sounded like a plea, or like a voice crying "hello" up to his window. He pictured a little girl in a lace dress with braids and barrettes at the bottom of the airshaft, who was locked out by accident, crying all night. He built up a story around her; she'd gotten lost years and years ago on a cold winter night, and now she was looking to make friends.

When Alex asked his mother if ghosts were real, she was scared for him. Children were more sensitive and vulnerable to the Aether—Alex in particular. As a baby, active Aether designs made him cry, and up until recently, he got dizzy every time he got too close to a ward.

His mother explained that sometimes when a person died, they left an imprint behind. It was dangerous for a healthy person to manipulate the Aether, but the dying had no such reservations. They could fuel one last command with their entire life without fear of consequences. The constructs they left behind were simple—most were harmless—but the ones that weren't could be easily taken care of.

But even after they talked, he woke up crying, thinking of the girl in the airshaft. He crawled into bed with his mother, waking her up only a few hours before she had to get up for work. To cut back on his nightmares, she tried putting his bed in the front room. He could hear traffic from the street all night long, but there was something reassuring about waking up from a nightmare and hearing business as usual on the street below.

He slept well for the rest of the year except for the one night the streetlights went out. He never told his mother that he woke up when the apartment was dark as a closet. From the bedroom, he heard a high-pitched voice call "Hello?" and saw two little points of light pierce through the darkness.

Chapter Seven

LOISAIDA TRIED TO plan her strategy for taking her inquiry to the Night Court. Jealous isolationists kept the courts too heavily divided to make open overtures, but even if she couldn't talk about a mutual problem without starting rumors, there were ways around talking to the court.

On her ride to her office, she brought up the number for the Committee for Paraterrestrial Collaboration. The Committee was an NGO dedicated to working between the United States Government and the various court systems in place across the country.

Her quick inquiry soon turned into an all-night project. Every person she spoke to passed her along until she felt she had spoken to everyone in their directory through their telephone transfer system. At last, she passed the thick crust of receptionists and office managers and reached a level within the company powerful enough to be suspicious of her. They quizzed her on her motives, jumped to wild conclusions, and accused her of espionage. Finally, after hours, she said her piece for the last time.

"I am the representative of the people of the Lower East Side. My constituents and peers refer to me as the Lady Loisaida, Death of Fire, the Carpenter. I am the natural heir to the northern portion of the Rio Maimon in the Dominican Republic. It has recently come to my attention that there are growing numbers of missing persons cases happening within the tristate area. I want to know where it started, when it started, how widely it's spread, and whether it can be contained."

She was answered with silence.

"I'm sorry. Can you repeat that?"

She repeated herself, "I want to know why there are people missing. In order to do that, I need information on the first identified case: when it happened, how often it's happened since, and whether anyone has stopped it."

More silence. "How often has it happened in your territory?"

"I'm not sure," Loisaida said. "But I need information on what is happening outside my territory as well."

"Our work with the courts prevent us from sharing information with Lords outside of their known alliances."

Loisaida grit her teeth. "I don't care how big other people's lands are, how many people are in them, or where they get their resources. I want information on a known phenomenon. Nothing else. Aren't there maps you can share without Lord's territories marked on them?"

For the first time that night, the person on the phone said, "Yes."

She was so happy she wanted to cry. "What do I have to do to have you share it with me?"

"Court peers can view our records, but it has to be done on our terms."

If she was told her handicaps in the first hour on the phone, she might have argued, but by then she was too relieved to complain. "Can I take notes?"

"Yes."

Once she'd set the appointment, she rewarded herself with lunch. While eating, she allowed herself to look over the work left behind by her interns. She paged through the paperwork on her desk absently, wondering when she'd have time to do anything but the missing persons investigation. The interns could handle the bulk of the office work—she made their job harder when she tried to help—but her territory would have to operate without her, and she didn't know if she could afford that. Ten years ago, she would have risked distancing constituents, but now she was vulnerable. There were new Heralds every day full of sweetness and desperation with proposals from their Lords. Developers were trying to build on her land without her permission, hundreds of new residents not paying her fealty, and predatory Lords lingering on her borders trying to gain support. If she drew away to work on this project, there would be people there to take advantage of her absence.

Looking at the challenges ahead made her wonder if there were failed investigations before her.

SAM SPENT ALL day looking for work and leads. She went to the highway to ask the Folk underneath for a way into the Tunnel systems, but they were bitter and silent. She asked a few tattoo shops in the area if they were looking for people, but they weren't. She went to Folk-run shops with her questions, but they acted suspicious. A fruit vendor, who swore he was really a raccoon wearing a lot of glamour, suggested something called the Bureau for Paraterrestrial Collaborations. When she finally went home, worn out from walking, she googled their number and worked meticulously through the automated questions to finesse the machine into connecting her to a person.

Once she reached the teller, she was told there was nothing they could do without personal information for a missing person. Not even an investigative organization could find a person with just their first name and ethnicity.

"If I did have all that, how would you guys find them?"

"Well, the case would have to go to the Police Department, Daytime Courts, and Nighttime Courts. Once they're alerted, we can work with them to begin a grassroots campaign—"

She hung up before hearing the remainder of the answer.

Sam spent the rest of the night on her phone, trying to shake answers out of the Internet. She rubbed her eyes and blinked the sleep back, but finally, she put down her phone to let a page load and let her eyes close a little too long, drifting off to sleep.

The apartment was warm and quiet—the only sound came from the humming of her lights. The silence and the warmth made her half-conscious mind ring with deep concern. She was alone, asleep somewhere without the usual sounds of snoring, Leticia's distinct, heavy sigh, or the usual low mumbling from those on the watch. She couldn't feel the floor under her, or the wind blowing through their camp. Where the hell was she, and why was it so stuffy?

She tried to take in her surroundings with her eyes closed; she was somewhere bright, warm, and so dry it made her nose hurt. She couldn't tell if she was alone. She tried to remember where she'd been before and gradually realized the places she thought of first were places she hadn't been in a long time. Just when she was on the verge of panic, floundering through memories without finding what she needed, it popped into her mind that she was at home and asleep on her bed. She relaxed, embarrassed, then sat up and rubbed the sleep out of her eyes.

The sky was turning blue as the sun rose, and below her window, her radiator was kicking up again. She forced open her old, tilted window and pulled the cold, dirty air into her lungs. The only thing to see outside her window was the air shaft and her neighbor's windows, which were mostly all boarded up with planks of wood, garbage bags, tape, patterned fabric, and air conditioners. The rest were blocked by shelves, knick-knacks, and tendrils of plants. She was the only one in the building who cracked the window from below instead of above. She took some small satisfaction in being the only one who saw the pearl-gray paint and small canvas of navy-blue sky.

The sharp image of dark, cold tunnels packed with earth came back to remind her that people were buried in the wet ground. She plugged her phone into the charger and went back to work.

NAILS WAS RESTLESS all morning. Alex could hear him pacing in the kitchen, scraping chairs back to stand up and dragging them forward to sit down again. When Alex got up hours later, Nails was sitting, tapping his feet and the fingers of his left hand while chewing on the thumb of his right.

"What's up?" He asked, but Nails just waved him off and went back to chewing. Alex made coffee and put together a breakfast from what little he had in the fridge, and noticed out of the corner of his eye that Nails was checking the time on his phone as if the minutes were crawling by.

Alex sat down across from him. Nails was chewing hard on his finger, gnashing his teeth at some imperfection on the cuticle too small for Alex to see. He seemed uncomfortable under Alex's scrutiny and turned away to stare at the wall.

"What's up?" Alex repeated.

Nails scowled and checked his hand. A red drop of blood beaded up from the bed of his nail. "I wanna talk to Miss LES."

"Why?" Alex asked. Nails didn't answer. "Today?"

He gave Alex a wild, manic look and nodded. Alex felt an anxious churn in his stomach. He did a tally in his head; Nails hadn't slept well in weeks, and while normally Alex didn't keep an eye on how well he was taking care of himself, he couldn't remember the last time he'd seen Nails take his meds. He wasn't sure he'd seen the little orange bottle in the Gross House at all.

Then again, Nails was smart, and when he said something was wrong, it usually was, even if he couldn't clearly explain what caught his attention.

"OK. I'm coming, too."

Nails stared him up and down as if trying to read his mind. He nodded, but his body language screamed suspicion. "OK."

They arrived at her office at five thirty. Nails sprinted to catch the door behind someone and beamed when they turned around to look at him. They could hear Loisaida's voice through the door, speaking with cold, measured anger to someone already in her office. When she answered the door, the sight of them made her freeze. Her face was stony.

"Perfect timing," she said at last.

She pushed the door open. There was a perfect mirror image of Nails already standing in her office. Same huge, staring eyes, same nervous shifting of weight. Both Nailses gave each other the same confused expression, both their hands in the pockets of their jeans, both their heads bent. They overacted their surprise by rearing up, then leaning in with both their hands in the pockets of their jeans and both their heads bent.

She slammed the door and made a point to get between them, raising her arm to protect the Nails Alex came with. "Time to cut the shit,"

"What the fuck is this?" Nails cried.

"This is not my fault!" the other Nails said.

"Don't play dumb," Loisaida warned, taking another step forward.

The Nails already in the office flung his hands out in exasperation, the same way Nails did. "Why not play dumb, isn't that the game we're playing?"

"This is fucking wild." the other Nails said.

Loisaida got a little closer. "One more chance."

Nails looked uncertain for a second, then squared his shoulders and leaned in. "Fuck you."

She cocked her head at him, as if waiting to see if he was sure. The Nails in her office stared back. Alex had been in enough fights with Nails to recognize the posture immediately. With his bottom lip between his teeth, his hands in his pockets and his eyes as wide as they could go, most people assumed he was too scared to fight back. He freely admitted that the start of every fight made him nervous, but that was natural. He was thinking. Alex glanced at the Nails by his side and saw the same expression, but different posture. He was sliding into a crouch, preparing to move fast. Alex followed the arrow of his shoulder to the desks across the office and shifted his weight.

Loisaida pulled something off the Nails that was standing in her office before them. Without moving, there was a ripple to the air like a sheet fluttering, then a loud crack. Nails's ankles twisted all the way around. He fell on his face and began to scream. His hair dissolved, and his knees popped and reversed in their sockets.

Even as the features of his face melted, Alex felt a gut-deep reaction. His feet moved without thinking, carrying him away from the creature as it melted in front of him.

"Goddamn piece of shit fucking *serpent!*" the Nails on the ground shouted as his skin stretched like putty around revolving rows of teeth. His arms turned over in their sockets like a doll's, and with all four limbs, he pushed off the floor and stuck to the ceiling like a lizard.

Alex hit the wall. The door was right next to him. He could leave, but before he could reach for the door, he caught sight of the remaining Nails, still crouched as if ready to run, but frozen and gaping.

"*Liar!*" Loisaida shouted at the creature crawling across the ceiling. "What do you want with these children?"

"What do *you* want with these children?" it demanded as it reached down for a window. The skin on its hand burst, raining blood on the carpet, and the hand retracted. "Fucking bitch!"

She was weaving something in the air, which made the air dry, brittle and hard to breathe. "Don't test me. I'm the representative of the Lower East Side, and I have these two under my protection. Now tell me what you want."

"Company," it said.

She made a gesture like pulling a thread, and it screamed again as the front of its shirt went dark with blood.

Move, Alex thought. The unmelted Nails took a step, but no more. Alex abandoned the door and lunged at him, dragged Nails behind the desk, then looked around for something like a weapon—chair, lamp, coffee mug, thick binder, or anything—but the chairs were all lightweight for easy moving and the lamps were all wall fixtures.

The only thing light enough for Alex to carry, but heavy enough to hurt, was the microwave and the coffee maker, and he had picked a desk too far to reach them. He opened drawers in the desk, but there was nothing in them except more paperwork. He took off his belt, wrapped the tongue around his hand, and left the buckle dangling studs out. Nails unlatched a chain and wrapped it around his knuckles.

There was a bang as the body dropped from the ceiling and landed on the floor. It spider-walked across the carpet too fast to catch. Nails dove out from behind the desk and rolled over to the water cooler.

The thing reached for Alex and closed its fist in air. A second hand came out of its wrist and snapped close enough to scratch his face. Loisaida made a forceful gesture and one of the thing's eyes collapsed in its socket. It screamed.

Nails whipped it with the chain in his hand and cut open the skin on its forehead. With a roar, it lunged forward with torso and arms stretching forward. Nails picked up the water cooler and slammed it down on the thing. Alex, running out from behind the desk, whipped his belt from behind.

"Get away!" Loisaida shouted. "Clear! Don't touch him!"

The thing helicoptered a leg out and slammed Alex in the stomach and sent him flying. For a second, he was too surprised to think. Then his back slammed into a row of filing cabinets. Spots flashed in his eyes. He blinked, trying to shake it off before the thing came after him. There was screaming all around him. He squeezed his fist to see if his belt was still in his hand and felt the studs dig into his palms.

The spots parted enough to see through. He didn't understand what he was looking at, then recognized Nails in the tangle of the fight. He was on his back, trying to push the thing off him as it raked long claws over his face. He was screaming. The thing's jaw split like an ants' mandibles and stretched out towards him.

Alex tried to stand, fell, tried again, gave up, and crawled. A wall of black muscle swept in front of him and shoved him back against the wall. Blearily, he looked around to see what new shit was flying at him and saw coils of scales standing two feet tall stretched across the floor. Loisaida appeared above them taller then he'd ever seen her. She wrapped her arms around the thing's neck, her tail around its legs, and squeezed.

"Let him go," she warned. It didn't answer. Its one remaining eye was focused on Nails.

Alex scaled the first half of Loisaida with every muscle throbbing. "Let him go, and you'll live."

"Fuck you," the thing wheezed.

Loisaida clenched her teeth and closed her arms tighter around its neck. It choked in thick, wet bursts.

"Get it off him!" Alex shouted. The thing took one hand off Nails to dig into Loisaida's arm. "Get it off!"

Loisaida stared at him with cold eyes. He reached into the mess of bodies and tried to peel the thing's fingers away from Nails. Something punched him right between his eyes, and he fell back. He touched his forehead and felt dampness—he was bleeding. A small mouth retreated back into the thing's empty eye socket and lashed the air with a tongue as strong as a whip.

"Stay back," Loisaida ordered.

"Fuck you," the thing said, then looked up at Loisaida. "And you."

It looked at Alex. "And you."

"You first," Alex snapped.

"Drop the boy," Loisaida ordered.

"Let me go or you'll never find him again," the thing said.

"That's the same as betting your life," she said, squeezing tighter. The creature made a dry, gurgling noise and shivered in her arms. Its head stretched and teeth snapped uselessly at her face before it deflated.

Her blank expression turned to horror as it slapped onto the floor like a wet balloon. She got it in both fists, but it sagged, opened a wet mouth, and let out a forlorn squeak.

She looked back and forth from the floor to Alex helplessly. "Help me!"

The wrinkled thing stretched out towards him like a snail reaching out of its shell. Loisaida lunged forward and grabbed what used to be its head. It squealed like a whistle, then stiffened, wrinkled, and dried like a sponge. Loisaida's eyes bulged as she strangled it, her teeth clamped shut. The length of it shriveled and dried down to thin, dried skin. When at last the thing lay lifeless on her floor, she stopped struggling and sat back with an exhausted huff.

"Where is Nails?" Alex asked. The floor was bare.

She pinched the bridge of her nose. "You know where he is."

Alex was still holding his belt. He could feel wet blood crusting on his wrists and stains on his coat and pants. He hurt. Copper filled his mouth.

"Are you OK?"

"What happened?" he asked again. When Sam disappeared, a whole train was ripped off the tracks, but Nails disappeared without a sign. He was there, and then he wasn't.

Loisaida let go of the dried rind of the thing on the floor and bent over him. "He was taken. Do you understand? They tried to take him hostage, but I turned the game around. It's fine—don't worry. I won't let this go any further."

"Where is he?"

"I'll find out," she promised.

Alex felt like she was trying to soothe him to make it easier for him to understand, but he knew what she was saying better then she wanted him to. He went through this with Sam a month ago.

She sank down, telescoping to the height he was used to seeing her, and a new pair of legs appeared beneath her.

"Why don't you know?"

"When people first started talking about the disappearance, I didn't think it was important. I'm looking into it, and I promise you I'll have more information for you. For now, please be careful tonight. Stay home, put up your block."

"We don't have one," Alex said. His stomach felt weird. Unnaturally hollow, as if it had turned to marble in his body and the cold stone was bruising all his other organs.

"Now's the time to get one," she said. "Go to the hardware store and get a cheap one for twenty bucks. Wait—I'll give you one of my herald shields. They're not much, but they keep negative attention off you."

She got a cardboard box out of a file cabinet and took out a small brass pin. The details on it were too small for him to make out, although it might have been a family crest. She pinned it to his jacket with a nervous but optimistic pat.

"Stay safe. Keep in touch. Call me if anything out of the ordinary happens tonight. I don't care if it's as small as a new cat in your neighborhood. Call me. Promise?"

"OK."

"Good. I'll call you tomorrow."

Chapter Eight

ALEX LEFT LOISAIDA in a daze. He half-hoped Nails might have been spirited back to Brooklyn, but he wasn't there. He gave Nails's phone a call, which went straight to voicemail. He should have called Nails's mother to tell her what happened, but he called Sam instead.

"You sure you're good alone?" she asked.

"Yeah." He needed the peace of isolation.

He left his phone on the bed and climbed into the shower. The warm water was less soothing then he hoped, stinging his cuts. The cuts themselves were surrounded by dark bruises and the edges bristled with lint.

He flipped his hair over to first dry his roots, and then the ends of his curls. When they were damp and springy, he experimented with hiding the bruised side of his face behind a curtain of hair, but to hide it all, he needed to cover his face.

Alex paused to fish a loose hair off his tongue and felt it catch somewhere in his throat. When he pulled, it dug into the soft flesh of his throat like a wire. He choked and stopped pulling, letting it rest. He paused to catch his breath. His reflection in the mirror was ruddy with effort, his eyes red and moist. He pulled again and felt the hair drag against his esophagus like a paper's edge. He felt a weight on the other end and pulled carefully, praying the hair wouldn't snap. The thin gossamer thread of blonde hair held, curls stretched flat to form in small peaks along the length. When he let them go, they sprung back into shape and wrapped around his fingers.

Another hair snaked out. He snatched it with his other hand and pulled, gagging. Another hair unraveled from around the first two and lay in a wet spiral against his wrist. Bleached, curly hair came swimming out of his throat, tickling the roof of his mouth. He imagined pulling himself inside out like in a cartoon. Soon, hair covered the sink. He was going to throw up. He didn't want to puke in the toilet and trail hair through the bowl. He thought about cutting it off, but a small portion of him worried there might be some witchcraft to make him confuse the hair with his tongue.

He was going to vomit.

Alex gagged twice and sprayed a mouthful of chewed rice into the wads of hair in the sink. He couldn't breathe, and his eyes felt like they were about to pop. His stomach contracted like someone was trying to squeeze the contents out of him. The taste of bile filled his mouth, and in a spray of spit, he coughed up a wet mass of curly, bleached-blonde hair. He wiped the last strands off his face and sat down on the toilet to catch his breath.

Slowly, he pulled himself up to wash again. As the cool water ran over his hands, he asked why, how, and who. He didn't know anyone with the skill to pull off something that specific from that far away, except for the Kijkaan, or Loisaida, and he dismissed her immediately.

Alex went back into the bathroom and looked down at the wet, stringy mess clogging the sink. He hated to call her again so soon, but she was the only person he had.

He thought the main room was empty, but on his way to his room, a chair moved back and the skinny redhead girl— Amy, the one who hid dirty dishes in her room— stood up. She looked longingly into the bathroom behind him.

He smiled as cheerfully as he could. "Can you give me one second? I need to clean up in there."

She looked like she was going to push the issue.

"Please?"

"OK."

He ran into his room and grabbed his phone off the bed and placed a call. When he came back, she was in the bathroom watching bubbles squelch in the hair casserole.

"Don't stand too close to that."

"It smells like vomit," she said.

"Yeah."

"It looks like—"

"Yeah, it looks like my hair," Alex said. Before he could make up an excuse, the call picked up.

"What looks like your hair?" Loisaida asked.

"Miss LES? It's Alex again. The fucking Basement Suit sent me another message."

"Basement Suit?" she repeated, then angrily, "A *message*?"

"I pulled two feet of my own hair out of my stomach. It's real. My roommate's looking at it right now."

A sharp silence. When she spoke, it was slow and hard. "Send me a picture."

"What's going on?" the redhead asked.

He ignored her and took the picture, holding his breath as the camera struggled to focus. He exhaled as the sink appeared in the picture splattered with hair looking as real as it had to him.

"That is a lot of hair," Loisaida said when she called back.

"I know!" he cried.

"Is it really all yours?"

"What else could it be?"

She made an uncertain noise. "Are you missing any hair?"

He reached back to feel his scalp. It didn't feel any different. "I don't know, whose else's hair would it be?"

She hummed. "It could be a wig, but-- the important thing is the photo gives you a timestamp. Save the rest. Do you still have that business card he gave you?" she asked without waiting for a response. "Bring it to me in the morning."

"Save it where?" he asked, but she hung up. He gave the Gross House a quick survey, returning to the bathroom when the redhead kept trying to use it.

"Don't you want it clean first?" he snapped, digging through the recycling bin for a glass jar big enough to hold his hair. He scraped as much of the soup into the jar as he could through two layers of protective plastic bags and wrapped the rest up for trash. As he pulled the hair hand over hand out of the drain, flecks of food scattering around him, he was amazed at how much his stomach could hold.

Of course, there was only one sponge in the kitchen, but he felt their old, overused dish sponge could provide one last service to the house.

When he was finally done, he found himself facing a group of different roommates standing in the kitchen. Usually he only saw two or three outside their rooms, but the redhead seemed to have gathered everyone together. Alex could remember details about their individual lives, but not a single one of their names came to mind.

The chubby white kid who worked in tech smiled. "Hey— it's Alex, right? Can you tell me what's going on?"

"Uh, well..." He quickly packaged the night into a digestible fact. "I clogged the sink and had to fix it."

"Mmm-hmm, that's what Amy told us. What happened?"

The redhead's name must have been Amy.

"It's kind of complicated and not really important."

"We're your roommates. You can talk to us."

He switched tactics. "You're right, and I will, but let me do it another time."

The tech kid nodded sympathetically. "Yeah, well, we thought now might be a good time to talk to you about the complaints we've been hearing."

"Complaints?" he repeated, shocked that he was the source of complaints and not the girl who brought loud, drunk friends home late at night, or the guy who routinely left pots of rice to burn on the stove. Or even Amy, who hid food in her room until it rotted. "What about?"

"Well, to start with, I understand you brought another person to live with you without talking to the rest of us."

He felt his stomach sink. He knew this was coming. "He's a friend of mine. Has he been a problem?"

"No problem, but how long is he staying?"

"Until he finds his own place," Alex said, which was the agreed-upon lie they came up with until one, or the both, of them found a better situation.

"And how long is that going to take?"

"I'm not sure."

"Because, you know, rent goes up if you add another person to the room."

His train of thought dissolved. He could only stare. *"What?"*

"We try to work as a team, and that means sharing the price of the rent and bills for this unit. So when someone needs a rent deduction, we work around them, and if they have a partner, say, move in with them, then we need to raise their rent to balance the rest of the house."

"But all the rooms are different prices."

The chubby kid cocked his head thoughtfully. "Yes, but if someone brings in a new person to the floor—"

"Then that means all the rents get adjusted."

The white kid smiled. "Not exactly."

Alex wasn't bad at math—or great—but that didn't add up. "So then somebody's skimming."

"No. All the money goes back into the house."

He could see it would be pointless to ask how. "Listen, bro, I'm the only one here who pays rent on time. Don't hit me up for more."

"We're not saying you're late on payments, we're saying—"

Alex dug in. "Is anybody late right now?"

"I don't see what that has to do with this," the white kid answered.

"Why is this the first meeting we've had when the lights have been out twice because of late bill payments?"

"We're working on that. But if you want to live here, then you need to live with us. I'm sure your friend is a great guy, and we won't make him leave, but we all need to adjust if you want to bring a new person in."

Alex stared at his closed-lip smile that crinkled his eyes in such a controlled and practiced way. Amy was standing with her back to the wall as if she was waiting for a fight to break out, and there was another guy on the other side of the tech kid with his fists at his side as if he was, too.

"OK," Alex said. The tension broke. People began going back to their rooms. Alex packed his and Nails's bags and left the apartment as soon as the path was clear.

THE SHEETS ON Nails's cot were still bunched up on his bed, twisted and stretched from his restlessness that morning. God knew how early he woke up, frustrated by Loisaida's inaction on Sam's case. It felt strange to stand in front of it without him there. The air was so stale that if Alex closed his eyes, it felt like Nails was still there. The room was close, whether or not anyone was in the room with him.

Nails said they met a few years before they started hanging out. He said he started talking to Alex because he always saw him around at shows and even spoke to him once or twice. Alex didn't remember Nails at all until the day he looped an arm in a cast around Alex's neck and shouted, "Hey! My dad's in jail! Who wants to *celebrate*?"

Alex naturally said no, but to his surprise, his friend Tatiana said yes, and he wasn't leaving her alone with some random guy bragging about jailtime. Nails hailed a cab, pulled out his phone, and started talking a mile a minute, first to tell his mom he was having some friends over, then to a dealer. It sounded like his mom was against having friends over because he shouted her down and hung up abruptly. He organized an entire party in the ten-minute ride it took to get from Union Square to 45th and 10th. He then marched them to the corner deli and bought three cases of beer.

"So, what happened with your dad?" Tatiana asked politely as they helped him negotiate the three cases of beer, his keys, and the broken arm.

"He's in jail!" he said proudly.

He led them up three flights of stairs to his apartment, which was one big square with two bedrooms and a closet built in. He went to a door with an enormous hole hacked into it and tried to open it, but the lock was jammed. Tatiana was shooting Alex worried looks but never made a move to leave. They were still there thirty minutes later, fighting with the door, when the crazy guy got a call that brought them all downstairs to let another friend in. Alex planned on slipping away while they were outside but stopped when he saw that the friend they were meeting was Sam.

"How do you know this guy?" he whispered as she hugged him.

She looked at him funny. "You don't?"

"Maybe you can help us out with this door situation," Nails said while galloping up the stairs. Instead, her eyes fell on the cases of beer at their feet.

"You're not going on a fucking bender," she said flatly.

"Why not? My dad is in jail—we have to celebrate!" He put a new bottle between his knees to pry the cap off. "So why'n'cha help us out?"

Sam grimaced and tried the handle, then put her shoulder into it. When that didn't work, she suggested breaking off the doorknob. They got a wrench from under the sink and pulled the knob off. Next, Tatiana suggested picking the lock. Sam handed her the doorknob lock first.

They worked through the beers while waiting for inspiration. The dealer arrived and followed them upstairs for a beer. He recommended the credit card trick, but after three school IDs and one debit card were bent, they gave up. Three of Nails's friends came—the original lineup for his band, Kwik-E-Leak—and tried to grease the door open with WD-40. By the time Chelsea and Desiree showed up, the door was still locked, and at that point, Sam lost her patience and put her boot through what was left of the door.

Behind the shattered door was a small room with too much furniture; there was a dresser, a bed, an air conditioner jutting out over the bed, and a couch all around one perfect square of green rug. They put the beers there and climbed onto the furniture. Tatiana lay sprawled across Alex, Desiree, and Chelsea's lap. Packrat was on the dresser. Nails was sitting on the bed and using the air conditioner like a table. Alex didn't keep a clear memory of the rest of the night, but he woke up the next morning on the dirty couch in Nails's room with a pounding headache and a dry throat. He found his shoes crammed under the couch and staggered out to freedom, where Nails was sitting at the table with Tatiana.

"You want some food?" Nails asked.

"No," Alex said, keeping his teeth clenched to hold back the waves of vomit crawling up his throat. "Not hungry. Should go."

"You should probably get some water in you, at least," Nails said. "You look kind of... waxy."

Alex wanted to reason with him, but instead dropped his shoes and ran to the bathroom, pushing up the toilet lid as the first spray of bile bubbled up.

When he was done, he crawled back into the sitting room and pulled himself into a chair. "What do you have to eat?"

From then on, Alex noticed Nails when he was out at shows. They talked, they hung out, and Alex met Nails's mother, Lisa—a small, thin white woman with curly black hair who wore a lot of dark colors and smoked thin white cigarettes as strong as pipe tobacco. She hated her son's nickname.

"It's so cruel. You shouldn't call him that. Honey, don't let them call you that."

"Why not?" Nails asked, chewing on his fingers as they talked.

"Is that how you want people to think of you? Is that how you want to think of yourself? You don't want that to stick, honey, names have power."

Alex learned Nails used to go to private school. He'd never met anyone who went to private school before.

"What was it like?"

"It was so dumb," Nails said, rolling his eyes. He was taught by professors who believed they were molding the minds that would run America. His family was far from equal to the titans of industry that raised his peers, but he kept pace with the workload. He made friends easily, took lacrosse, and even made a winning score.

Then he noticed he wasn't feeling well. At first, he thought it was physical, but as it dragged on and on, he realized it wasn't something that was going to be fixed with a few days off. Nothing he did seemed to release the pressure in him and the stress burst at odd times. He broke all the glasses in the cabinet. He started yelling in the street one day. Things appeared in his vision that other people didn't see. Battle Row refused to check if someone hexed him, but a specialist said it wasn't metaphysical.

The next step was to see psychiatrists. They suggested it was depression and told them to put him in a juvenile facility for a few days and see if he felt better. He spent an extra-long weekend at a facility and ended the experience with a new prescription for anti-depressants.

Two weeks later, he blacked out in class and woke up in the hospital. He'd bitten off the nail on his thumb.

People treated him differently after that, and over the next year, he spent more time in the hospital then he did in class. He was placed on probation and strongly suggested to find a different school.

The next year he was enrolled in a different school but missed the first day of class. Then, the second. He told his parents he would rather get his GED.

"And then what?" his dad asked. "You don't have the credits for early college enrollment. What are you going to do, be a fisherman like your Zaydee?"

"Worked for him," David said.

His dad responded by putting Nails's head through a door.

Alex became familiar with the Kaczorowskis' divorce through Lisa's sad, quiet moments. He learned Lisa had Nails while she was still in college. She thought she was lucky to have such a good relationship with the guy that got her pregnant, so she navigated all the worst parts of an unplanned pregnancy by sending Nails to his grandmother in Westchester. Nails had no memory of his first years with his grandma, but he remembered subsequent memories, idyllic ones in a sleepy suburb full of grass and trees.

After the Kaczorowskis landed their first jobs, they moved to Hell's Kitchen to be in the middle of everything. They became the very first wave of gentrification on their block, a perspective Alex suggested and Lisa rejected, pointing out that they got to know their neighbors, shopped in local stores, and let Nails play on the playground with the neighborhood kids.

Alex was there when Lisa noticed their rent checks weren't being cashed. She was short that month after paying her lawyer's fee and was monitoring her bank statements with extra care to make sure she wasn't overdrawn. The next month, after some careful budgeting, she sent the building management two checks; one for the current month and another for the previous month. When neither were cashed, a red flag went up in her mind. After management ignored three more payments, they served her paperwork for six months of unpaid rent.

The judge ruled in her favor, but management appealed. When Lisa arrived in court a second time with her lawyer and her stack of paperwork, management came with a complete report of Lisa's entire renting history on their property. They brought up every 911 call the Kaczorowski family ever made, forced Lisa to bring in copies of her son's mental health history and the restraining order she filed against her husband. For a few months, they tried to convince the court that Lisa Kaczorowski was running an illegal single room occupancy in her apartment using footage from the security camera to show her son leading 'suspicious characters' into the building. Alex and Sam were in the footage. The judge clucked and shook his head like the Kaczorowskis were rats in a box, tearing each other apart. If the trial was fair, the landlord's shoddy evidence would have been quietly pushed off the table, but the landlord's judge took less than a week to rule in his favor and gave the Kaczorowskis a month to move out.

Alex was there when they found out about the court's final decision.

"Is this real?" Nails asked.

Lisa said nothing.

While she packed, Lisa reached out to her friends. None of her contacts had space for her or the time needed to make space. Lisa swept twenty years of her life into storage and found a sublease on Craigslist. She didn't have time to get comfortable before she moved to another sublease, then another after that. Each month her subleases and storage tore through her paycheck, and she hated chasing down subleases.

She needed a place to stretch out, relax, and meditate. If she couldn't have that, then the next best thing was someone her age she felt she could trust. At last, she breached a social boundary and called her son's best friend's mother for help.

Natalia Martinez, mother of Alex Delatorre, was surprised to hear from her. All their contact had been compressed into one ten-minute phone conversation a year before, which only happened because Alex kept coming home from his friend's house, smelling like he hadn't been near an adult in weeks. He always insisted that he just watched TV at Nails's house, but she didn't believe him until Lisa gave her the same answer. Lisa explained that she had a laissez-faire style of parenting, which preferred giving the kids the freedom to drink and smoke in the safety of her house rather than out on the streets somewhere.

She didn't get the sense that Natalia liked her much, but when she approached her about renting out Alex's old room, they saw each other as reliable resources.

The house on Staten Island would never replace the Hell's Kitchen apartment, isolated as it was from the City, but it had a backyard, and the island had its points of interest. There, she never had to worry about the men in her life, or budget expenses for protection, lawyers, or doctors. No drunk people screaming on her block. No Lord fights. No old wiring. Just two older women easing into retirement.

Chapter Nine

ALEX ARRIVED OUTSIDE the high chain-link fence around his mother's house, struggling to balance two bags full of their belongings. When he buzzed the bell, Lisa answered with surprise. "Alex, honey, how are you? How have you been? Where's that son of mine, didn't he come with you?"

He cringed. "Can I come in?"

"Of course, honey, it's your mother's house." She stepped aside and let him drop the bags onto the floor. "What's going on? Isn't it working at that place you were staying at?"

"No."

"Well, where's my son? Why's he not helping you?"

"He's....missing."

Her face fell. "What do you mean? What happened? Oh my god, did he...don't tell me...he had an episode?"

"No," he said quickly and then tried to explain. She listened in silence, then went to the back door, put on a coat and a pair of shoes, and began to smoke through the open door.

She toyed with her cigarette. "I'm not familiar with Senator Loisaida. Interesting name. I've met so-called kings and queens, but never a senator. Funny. So she's looking for him?"

"That's what she said."

She nodded and took a drag on her cigarette. "Your mother has a very good block on this house. Best I've ever seen."

"She does?" Alex asked, confused.

Lisa squinted at him through the smoke. "You didn't know? Hmmm, maybe she told you, and you were too young to understand. Maybe she hasn't got around to telling you yet. Why don't you go upstairs and talk to her? I need a second to think."

ALEX FOUND HIS mother in bed with her laptop resting on her knees, squinting at the screen through reading glasses. She looked so much smaller and older then he remembered, and while everything in the room was familiar, it seemed so much more distant than before, like a stranger's room.

There was the Gothic Cabinet Craft bookshelf she bought for their Harlem apartment, the beautiful, faux-vintage oak chest she dragged home from the curb, and an action figure he threw out in a purge of all his childhood belongings.

When she saw him in the doorway, she closed the laptop and dropped the reading glasses on the bed. "Blonde again?"

He put his hand in his hair. "No, I'm letting it rest."

"Good. Those chemicals are bad for you." She opened her arms.

He gave her a hug and sat down on the space she made on the bed.

She fixed the stray hairs around his face. "Have you been working?"

"No."

"Why not?"

He gave a shrug that was more of a bristle. "I'm not getting called back."

"You haven't just been sending them your resume, right? You at least gave out a few in person?"

"Most places ask you to e-mail them a resume," he said, sensing tension building.

"That doesn't matter, they need to see your face to know you're a real person."

They had had this exact argument many times before, and he wasn't interested in having it again. "Mom, I lost my apartment."

She stopped short in the middle of forming a sentence. The tension evaporated. "What do you mean? Why?"

"They tried to make me pay more money."

"What do you mean, more money? More money every month?"

He nodded.

Her wide eyes narrowed. "Are you on the lease?"

"No."

She hissed. "Do you have another place to go, or are you asking me if you can live here again?"

"I don't have a job; I can't pay a deposit. I can't even pay the first month's rent at a new place," he said and added hesitantly, "And Dave is missing."

She pushed herself up in bed. "What do you mean, missing?"

He gave her a different version than he told Lisa, editing their trip to the tunnel and his involvement in the fight. She listened, only responding with a stiff adjustment of her legs.

"I don't know what to say," she said when he was finished.

"I didn't expect you to have an answer."

"Yes, but"—she looked down at her legs—"can I ask you a question?"

She'd never warned him one was coming before. "OK."

"Is he your boyfriend?"

He rolled his eyes. "No, mom, he's straight."

"He doesn't look straight."

"Mom!" he cried. "What does straight look like?"

"Don't get mad at me. You're sleeping here tonight."

He bit his tongue before he asked what his other options were. "Thank you."

"The only space free is the couch. You know my day starts at five a.m."

"Yes, mom."

"Good. The sheets are in the closet. I love you, but I need to sleep."

"OK. Thanks, mom," he said, slowly backing out of the room.

"If you want to stay, you need either a job or to get enrolled in school."

He hated the implication that he wasn't looking for a job but swallowed his pride. "Fine."

She pointed at him. "Those are my conditions; either you help pay the bills, or you go to school. No exceptions."

"I said, OK. Damn."

She slotted her glasses back over her nose. "Thank you. I love you."

Chapter Ten

NAILS CLOSED HIS eyes as a twisting mass of flesh dug its claws into his face.

He opened them again to darkness.

He lay on a cold, hard surface, and there was a slight breeze passing over his face. He wondered briefly if he was dead and then if this was some kind of trick. He blinked but didn't notice a difference between eyes closed or open until he reached into his pocket and opened his phone. The light cast a glow around his body—a little window to normalcy in the situation he was in. It told him he had no service and the time.

He rose slowly. Nothing meaningful changed about his situation; he was still in the dark, still lost, but now he was upright. He was alone in a strange place with no belongings or way to escape. There was nothing but him and the soft, unknown darkness.

He began to walk. He wasn't sure of a rescue, so he took small and careful steps forward, testing the ground beneath him before putting his weight down. He thought that if he didn't use the flashlight on his phone, he could save the battery until he could use it, but he found himself checking it for the light.

Hours passed. Hunger clenched his stomach, and thirst coated his tongue, but he still stopped twice to pee. His legs felt stiff and heavy compared to the light hollowness of his stomach. He thought about sleep, but he didn't know if it was safe to sleep here unprotected. The battery on his phone ran into the red, and his heart pounded in his chest. Now he would lose the last glimmer of light he had and his only hope of connecting to the world above.

Before he could have a panic attack, he noticed a light in the distance. It was a faint orange glow like a birthday candle, but with so much darkness all around him, it looked as solid as a mark on a page. He reached out to see if he could touch it, but all he saw were the silhouettes of his fingers. He walked toward it and noticed the terrain was rough in that direction, tripping him while the light climbed higher on the horizon. It disappeared completely behind the ridge of the cliff.

He walked around the cliff one way, then the other, wondering if this was the kind of structure you could only reach from the air. To his surprise, the light seemed to rise like the sun at the other side of the cliff, and around a corner, at the bottom, he found gently sloping stone stairs. The climb was long, and he was so tired he made most of it on his hands and knees. He wondered if he should stop for the night right there on the stairs, but the fear of death motivated him to keep going.

When he made it to the top, he saw that the lower jaw of the cliff was bordered by a railing, streetlights, and a sidewalk—like any street in Queens. There were a few three-story brick buildings with a plot of dirt in front of each one. He went to the closest door and knocked, but no one answered. He saw three doorbells installed in the frame and rang each one. After a few minutes of waiting, he heard floorboards creak, and short, shuffling footsteps approached the door. An enormous alligator opened it, standing on two short back legs, with a hide riddled with bullet holes.

He was temporarily caught speechless. "Hi," he said eventually.

It gave him no indication that it heard him but stood and stared like it was sunning itself on a shore in Florida.

"I need some help."

The gator still didn't move. Nails felt a little out of his depth. Common sense said not to take free food from trasgo, and whether this gator counted as or not, he didn't want anything given to him by an animal that could live in liquid shit and eat raw meat.

"I'm looking for a market," he said finally. Markets were safe. Without fundamental safeguards against selfish behavior, they couldn't exist. He could establish boundaries and pay to have them respected.

Without hesitation, the alligator pointed one claw down the road.

"Thanks."

He followed the road into a tunnel in the face of the rock. A few feet in, the streetlights stopped, but that darkness was nothing compared to the cavern behind him. After another long stretch of darkness, the other end brightened up, and he walked into a small room with a high, jagged rock ceiling. The space was so small that a few vendors were selling out of backpacks. On the other end of the market was a hotdog stand—not one of the chrome ones he was used to but a big wooden cart with curls of peeling red paint under an umbrella so old and rotten the shredded fabric looked like lace. He walked straight up to it and put a dollar on the counter.

"Water," he said. The troll manning the cart reached into the cooler and gave him a bottle just like any other hot dog stand. He drank half of the bottle in the first long sip, finished it in the second, and came up for air gasping.

The water hit his stomach so fast it felt like ice. He bought two hot dogs, ate them without tasting them, then picked a flat piece of earth on the other side of the market and immediately fell asleep.

LOISAIDA WAS SCHEDULED to go to the Paraterrestrial Office on the same night her office was attacked. She did her best to clean up and throw away the chunks of ceiling, but smaller pieces of plaster got rubbed into the rug. The footprints on the walls and ceiling needed a professional cleaner, and she'd have to tell their landlord about the holes in the wall.

This was exactly why she had such a hard time finding office space.

She fixed herself up and took a cab to the Bureau office downtown, where she was scanned and patted down, then brought into a conference room with a small stack of paperwork, a USB drive, and a laptop. An agent explained that the USB drive carried maps, graphs, news articles, and other online media the Bureau found relevant to her search. The files contained the Bureau's collection of civilian and court complaints. The laptop was not connected to the internet—it was only there to help her view the material on the drive. Once the agent was satisfied that Loisaida understood her handicaps, she left the room, leaving the door ajar. Loisaida took a notepad out of her pocket, pulled the files towards her, and began to work.

On the USB drive was a time-lapsed map of New York and New Jersey, color-coded with overlapping blobs of blue, red, and green. She could zoom in or out of any spot to find more details on an event, or turn on the slideshow feature to watch a timeline of the reports appear on the map in sequence. They appeared in red when they were first reported, cooled down to blue over time, then stood out in green under new waves of red.

Events came and went all across the map as she toggled through eight months' worth of time. The report was made up primarily of missing persons cases, but included were reports of vanishing transit equipment, doors in previously blank walls, the time of day changing from one side of a building to the next, hallways leading to strange new places, and phantom windows hanging several yards over the roofs of buildings. At first, Loisaida didn't understand why she was given such a random collection of calls, but on a second read, after highlighting the notes left by the compiler, she found the thread of logic stringing it all together.

Each complaint, in some way or another, featured the transfer of space.

Complaints about the transfer of space were tricky because the concept of "space" itself had such loosely-defined parameters. The boundaries of a space had to be set by skillful Aether design, which gave direction to the unstable, limitless force called the Aether. The parameters for Inside a particular space had to be set by an engineer because the Aether had no mind to understand details like walls, roads, mountains, or water. Age-old superstition said that the Aether's disregard for property lines or bodily integrity made in-between spaces particularly dangerous, but the truth was more complicated when the borders of a city or country fluctuated over time, as much as the walls of a house, the borders a field, or the roots of a tree. Not even the structural integrity of a solid could be relied on indefinitely, but in order to guess some of the consequences of an action, an engineer needed to imagine the world from the perspective of a universal constant.

At the end, with the note pad full, she stopped to breathe. She came with the intention to read through everything twice, but she couldn't find the energy.

After lunch and some light work on another project, she took the notepad out of her purse and read it again. A fresh eye on her notes brought her to new questions about the Bureau's catalog of complaints. If the City was refusing responsibility for any Aetheric phenomenon, and the courts were given restricted access, at best, then who was investigating it? It was clear by the neat order of the files that the Bureau felt there was enough of a problem to study it and enough of a pattern to map it out, but for what? If there was an ongoing investigation within the Bureau, wouldn't they re-direct her to them? Not if they were working with the City. But if the City was involved, why did both the mayor and the governor refuse to answer questions about the disappearances? Why would the NYPD officially hand over responsibility to the courts?

Only someone with a direct connection to the phenomenon and enough of an understanding of Aetheric theory could answer her questions. Alex and his friends weren't qualified to explain specifics about the phenomenon, but the Kijkaan—

She didn't want to talk to him, but she knew she must. First thing tomorrow, she'd call Alex.

She opened a drawer, which pulled out farther and farther, building the Aether hum into a sustained, ghostly note. At the bottom of the drawer, now stretched halfway across the floor, was the petrified flesh of the shapeshifter.

She pierced her finger and squeezed two drops of blood on it. The dry, crinkled skin absorbed it instantly and began to thicken and puff, like bread in an oven. It twitched and gasped for air like a man dying. The muscle under its skin rippled and bulged, then rocked tentatively, testing its boundaries. Loisaida dug her nails into it until it flopped back listlessly.

A little pink human tongue appeared at one end and licked square human teeth. "What day is it?"

She did not answer.

The lump of flesh gave a small, shivery sigh, as if catching its breath. "What do you want?"

"Answers to the questions I already asked you," Loisaida answered. "Who is your Lord, and where is that kid you were shaped like?"

It wheezed. "It doesn't matter. He's a loser. He'd disappear one day, in one way or another."

She reached back into the drawer and squeezed. "Where is he?"

"Underground," it gasped.

"Where? Is he in one of the old train lines, the Croton reserve, the lake— where?"

"I can't narrow it down. They're building new infrastructure all over the City."

"Good enough. Who's your Lord?"

"You wouldn't understand—"

"I don't care."

It shuddered and slowly turned over. "The Lord Bullrush of the East End still claims my family loyalty, but—"

"—Bullrush hasn't been in the City since the thirties."

"Exactly." It hesitated briefly, either to suck in more weak breathes or to plan its next sentence. "I work for the Lord of Thundertown."

"Sounds ominous," Loisaida said mildly. "I've never heard of him."

"It's a new title."

Intimidating names were part of the job. Nobody ever maintained a steady career as Lord Bob from Hempstead, but if Bob became Lord Hempstead, borrowing a name from something greater than himself gave him an air of legend. Of course, the change brought challenges as well as renown, as scrubs from far and wide came to test each Lords' prowess.

She couldn't understand why anyone would make a title to control the Tunnels. When she was a kid, watching petty Lords rise and fall was like watching the weather. There were too many people living there, each more desperate and frightened with every passing day. Sometimes new Lords were destroyed before a challenger had time to rise.

"Who managed to unite Thundertown?"

"I don't know."

"Wasn't it your boss?"

"No, it was the Lord."

Loisaida reigned in her impatience. "Who's the Lord?"

The flesh under its skin bubbled as it twisted thoughtfully. "I don't work directly with the Lord."

"Who *do* you work with directly?"

"The Kijkaan," the shapeshifter muttered. There was a subtle change in the air as a new Design activated outside of and around the blocks and shields on her office. She could feel the keyhole opening, giving the Kijkaan access to her office, and wondered mildly why the shifter didn't invoke his name as soon as it woke up.

"I know you're listening," she said to her empty office. "You got my attention. I hope it was worth it. I will speak with you in one form or another."

She caught the strings of Aether between her fingers and drew the moisture out once again. The shifter let out a pained, ragged gasp, dried, flaked and shriveled, and fell silent. She closed the drawer intending to finish the work she'd neglected all night. When the phone rang, she answered it like she always did.

"Senator Loisaida's office, how can I help you?"

"You must be the East Village Lord," a deep voice said on the other side.

"I'm the most senior representative for the Lower East Side. Who is speaking?"

"You know me as the Kijkaan, and I prefer that name for professional purposes," the voice answered. "I see you were speaking to my messenger just now."

"I was hoping to find out which of his actions came from his own judgment."

"She," the Kijkaan corrected. "And I don't send my messengers out with the intention of having them held against their will."

Loisaida brushed the comment off. "She attacked me in my own office in the shape of a human. I couldn't assume her intentions were good."

"Really! That's surprising," the Kijkaan said. "I can't speak for her, but as her employer, I can only assume that she was acting in self-defense."

She scowled. "She contacted me on false pretenses and wouldn't drop them, even when confronted with her own falsehoods. I feel justified in distrusting her. Regardless of her intentions, and your expectations, you're her employer and you sent her to talk to me."

"Let's not throw accusations at each other; we both have justifiable reasons behind our actions. The only way to come to an understanding is through communication. I have no intention of storming your office to liberate her, so I cede to your authority and judgment. Now, I sent her to connect with you about a project I've been participating in—"

She cut him off. "Building a new city."

"Basically. The human city is ill-suited to a varied Alvar population. Any slight variation from the average human body puts us at a disadvantage, and many of us require circumstances for our health— such as damp soil, or a clean body of water— that are absent from city planning." he said and cleared his throat. "There are many differences between the Alvar population and Humanity, and they make it difficult for us to live in the City. We've only seen a few token concessions made for our comfort, while acres are deforested for theirs. We've waited long enough for Humans to adapt to us; I propose we take a different approach."

"So this is a militant proposal."

"But it isn't," the Kijkaan said, almost eagerly. "We shouldn't be forced to make any more shallow compromises, but we don't need to break the world in half. No more waiting, or planning, or arguing with a population with notoriously short memories. My co-producers and I believe that community creates mutually beneficial aid. Population clusters like Alvarville—also known as Thundertown—help foster that togetherness, but to create community, we need to address the glaring issue of governance. In the past, the Tunnels were prone to internal violence, as a result of mixed living conditions, and—"

"Get to the point," she interrupted.

"Of course." His tone was as sweet and sticky as honey. "No one person has ever managed to unite the Thunder Tunnels or held power there for long. The circumstances of the tunnels couldn't allow for it, but times are different. Lords no longer send their exiles there, migrant Alvar aren't pressured into moving there. People aren't ashamed to live in Thundertown. Tourists came while it was open. It's clear that the community is ready for the next step, to be a legitimate neighborhood within the City. They need a Lord who can build a modern, urban living space from nothing, and represent them in the Alvar Courts, but what one person can do that? None. It has to be a group effort. The solution is to share the title collectively, balancing the strengths and weaknesses of specialists into one bureaucratic entity."

Loisaida found herself surprised. It was true, no individual could schedule building contractors, make arrangements with the courts, and appear for mayoral meetings at the same time. Established Lords of the Court didn't need to build anything, but a Lord of Thundertown would need to fulfill centuries of development. It made sense to have a committee serve the community. She'd campaigned for a more open court system for years, arguing that treating Lords like they had divine rights was pointless when the Lordship was no longer a birthright.

"So you're telling me the Lord Beneath is a committee that acts as one entity."

"Correct."

"Which means no member of the collective will have any accountability for their actions."

He only hesitated briefly. "That's the way things have to be, but one day, I want us to go public with the collective. Gradually, we can acclimate people to the idea that we do all the work of a Lord, but our current members all hold seats in the court, and keeping it closed protects them from internal violence."

The courts were full of greedy, manipulative power players, but Loisaida didn't want to accommodate them with the intention of making plans for a better future. She wanted to make plans and put them into action— whether they failed or succeeded depended on factors outside of her control. Hiding behind a proxy struck her as insincere.

The Kijkaan continued, unconcerned by her silence. "I can send you our complete proposal when the mail goes out tomorrow morning, but I can give you highlights now. There are people in the collective who are inexperienced with peer groups, so we established a series of rules that will act as a base standard. For example, we discourage any physical violence. We treat any injury to an individual as an injury to the board and vice versa. No land will be disputed by board members, nor will territories be infringed upon. We want every individual within the group to be treated with respect so that they, in turn, will respect the group. Each member of the cooperative will benefit from the full rights and protection of the group, as well as shared ownership of the Lordship. In return, each prospective member will donate below-ground territory to the board."

"Which they would then become partial owner of," she said, fighting to keep the disapproval out of her voice.

"Exactly!"

"And who chairs this committee? You?"

He chuckled. "It's rotational, actually."

"Hmm." It wasn't obvious what the catch was, where the grift was hidden, but perhaps she could dissect it from the paperwork tomorrow night. "I have a few of my own questions."

"Please," he said, sounding eager.

"Immediately after I restrained your herald, one of my constituents pulled a wad of his own hair out of his stomach."

"Regrettable," he answered. "However, I only know three of your constituents."

"I'm aware. Of the three of them, one was transported underground by your herald, while she was dressed like him, and another experienced a very painful curse."

He paused. "Well— that's not my fault."

"I think it is. And the courts don't care what *you* think," she said coldly.

When he spoke again, his tone was sharp. "I don't like being threatened."

"And I don't like threatening people. I think it destroys when I need to build. We both need something from each other, so if you want us to work together, I recommend you find that boy your herald disappeared, and open exits to Thundertown that anyone can access."

The Kijkaan choked. "Absolutely not. That would put more people in danger than it's worth."

"People are already in danger," she said. "And my understanding is that you're not only aware, but participating in an effort to fix that. My constituents told me there was a list with several thousand complete names on it in your office."

"They aren't complete names," the Kijkaan said quickly. "Legal names only, in standard American format. First and last."

"Do you know why people are disappearing?"
He cleared his throat. "Ah, yes. I do."

Her grip on the phone tightened. "Is it one of the risks of giving below-sidewalk territory to your board?"

"Calm down," he soothed. "There's no need to get upset. Our first act as the Lord was to connect isolated residents of Thundertown. The first part of building community is building roads. Soon we'll have families sustaining a middle-class."

"But that is the future," she hissed. "What about now?"

"What I'm saying is our work came with consequences. That's the nature of work. At the same time, we have a method for connecting those who become Lost with an easy method of getting home."

"Do you know where any of those people pay their fealty?" she demanded, jabbing her finger in the air. "Do you have any information about them, besides their names? Where is this information coming from? Why haven't you shared it? Regardless of what you're trying to build with your committee, there is an epidemic of missing persons cases in the City right now that is going unaddressed because of how atomized our political structure is. You can't build a solution without telling anyone, or you're not accomplishing anything."

"All my information comes from public records. It's not my fault if other people can't do their own jobs. We have to balance so many plates to keep the whole city from sliding into the ocean. We're doing everything we can, but we can't undermine any of the work that's already finished—"

She didn't let him finish. "If you want to build a new borough, then it needs some way to connect to the rest of the City. What is your solution to getting people to work every day?"

"We're still laying infrastructure! Transportation is going to take more time to prepare."

"Well, we need emergency exits. That's an OSHA requirement—I can call the City right now for a stop-work order. If you don't want me to keep threatening you, then you need to make your project airtight."

"I can't do that. I'm not doing that," he said quickly.

"Consider your position," Loisaida continued. "I don't know who you've got on your board, but I know you have no title, and that you're signing your name on leases for territories with Lordships. You have files on serfs in territories you don't live in or work in. Think how easy that is to spin. Cooperate with me, and we can make this a nice, easy transaction; I'll give my portion of Manhattan Island to the collective, and you'll still seem like a champion for the underdog."

The Kijkaan laughed. "You can't do that. Who'd believe you? Why would they believe you?" There was a loud thump, as if he'd hit something. "Why wouldn't they believe *me* if I argued back?"

Loisaida didn't smile, even though she could feel one forming. "If it were to turn into a case of he said-she said, there would have to be an investigation."

The Kijkaan paused, chewing over his thoughts.

"Fine." The phone abruptly disconnected. Loisaida closed her eyes. She considered herself to be an extremely level-headed woman. It was a point of personal pride, tempered with the understanding that anyone could be called level headed in a career that rewarded brute force and flashy displays of power. She saw difficult moments as tests of resolve; nothing more.

When she looked out her window at the blank wall of the power plant, she felt content. Her pride was soothed;

she'd won the argument. She'd deal with whatever petty revenge the Kijkaan was planning.

SAM SPLIT HER day between looking for work and looking for leads and came out of a bar on Avenue A after looking and failing for some of both as three columns of smoke twisted up to the sky.

The cloud spread and collapsed above the rooftops, leaving a powdery smell in the air. Curious, she followed it, weaving through buildings, until she could taste the fine white ash on her tongue. The last rays of watery orange sunset reflected off the fog, twisting in the wind like a scarf. Coming up D on 9th, she saw red emergency lights flickering. The orange sunlight was gone, replaced by lamplight that stood out stark and distant. A crowd blocked the street, leaning over the police barricades to see better, selfie sticks jutted above. The cops leaned their hips on the joints of the barricades to watch the action.

Sam turned sideways and winnowed shoulder-first through the crowd to reach the front. The view from the barricade was guarded by dedicated onlookers, holding the barricade with both fists. Before them were three buildings with their facades torn off and spread on the sidewalk, exposing the apartments like a dollhouse. The ambulances were parked three-deep on the street, two wheels each on the sidewalk.

The Card House was down the street, and she cut around the block to check on it. The building looked undamaged from the outside, but she rung a few doorbells to be sure. No one answered their intercom, which didn't worry her immediately since there was always something broken, but when ten minutes passed and no one poked their head out the window, she pounded on the door with the flat of her fist.

The door opened a crack and Bonnie stuck her nose out. Her expression changed from furious to surprised. "Sa-MAN-tha! What are you doing here?"

"I saw what happened," she said. Through the door, she saw why no one answered their buzzer; everyone in the house was on the ground floor, some on chairs, others with their legs hung through the banisters, more pressed against the wall. "Came to make sure everyone was OK— what's going on?"

"We're having a meeting," Bonnie said, bringing Sam inside. "We're all fine— nobody died. Everybody's been calling, but we're all fine, it was all the way down there. The only thing we got to worry about is all this dust in the air."

Sam gave a nod to Erica, Paul, and Tom, and the people in the house she hadn't met. A few nodded back, but many held her stare.

A tall, skinny black kid dressed in clothes of clashing patterns spoke up. "We're talking about what we're going to do with the big hole in the basement."

"The what?"

Bonnie nodded at the stairs. "Go look, if you want. We need to finish up."

"We can't keep arguing again and again when we all know the clear answer is to call the Bureau," Erica said impatiently, gathering her skirt as she stood up.

"We are not calling the Bureau," Bonnie said.

Erica stopped on the stairs. "I'm not going to wait for this to become a bigger problem."

"Well, we're not calling the Bureau."

"Yes, we are."

"No, we're not."

Sam cut through the argument before it could get worse, upsetting chairs and bumping shoulders to squeeze through the basement door. The cold, clammy stairs, the cracks in the wall, the sharp smell of mold were all deeply familiar. The rusted collection of bike frames beneath the stairs, there as long as anyone could remember, were right where they always were. The most dramatic change of all was the gaping tunnel leading into darkness.

The walls of the basement were undamaged; not even the paint was chipped. The concrete floor ended where the tunnel began in a clear, straight line like they were pushed together. She tested the border with a plank of wood, and when nothing happened to it, took a few steps in. The inside was full of the same cold, rough stone as the outside, with nothing but more twisted rock as far in as she could see.

She climbed up the staircase and eased open the basement door to the safe, banal sight of a household argument.

Some blonde she never met, the third person under thirty in the room, managed to speak out above everyone else. "No— no— we can't wait for the lawyer to answer our calls."

"Well I'm not letting anybody come in here until we review our rights," Bonnie shouted.

"Come on, Bon—"

"No, YOU come on! I've been here for twenty years, how long have you been here?"

Sam cupped her hands around her mouth to shout. "What about Loisaida?"

"Who's Louise?" a voice shouted from the stairwell.

"*Who?*" Bonnie demanded.

"Loisaida. The Lord— the representative," Sam repeated. "She helped out with the lawsuit way back in the when. She could tell you your rights, and help with this."

"Loisaida, the street? The poem? The neighborhood?"

"I think she means the Lord."

"I know about her. She's cool. I have a friend who got her help," the black kid piped up.

"But we don't pay her fealty." Bonnie shot back.

"My friend doesn't pay her, either," the black kid said.

"We didn't pay her when she helped with the court case," Paul added, rubbing his chin thoughtfully. "She sent the judge proof of negligence without asking for money."

"She helped me, even though I'm outside of her territory," Sam said.

The blonde pressed harder. "It's a compromise; this is someone that we trust from the neighborhood, who we've worked with before, and who we have friends in common. We couldn't look for a better solution."

Bonnie's mouth twitched. "Fine."

Chapter Eleven

ALEX SNUCK BACK into the Gross House at two in the afternoon, a time he was pretty confident most people would be working. Now that he'd made peace with being back under his mother's roof and playing by her rules, he was looking forward to the benefits of living there. No more roaches, no more weird smells, no more food disappearing before he could eat it, and more food he didn't have to cook himself. Maybe he'd listen to her and try going to college one more time.

He was gathering up the last of his belongings while thinking smugly how glad he was he hadn't paid the rent that month when his phone rang, a sound so sharp in the silence of his room it made him flinch. He answered it crouched in the corner, trying to muffle his voice from the surrounding rooms. "Hello?"

"Hey, Alex, it's Sheldon. Um. How are you?" Magi said.

His teeth ground together. "I'm fine."

"OK, that's good. Did you get my text message?"

"No."

"Oh. I wanted Loisaida's number. I think an Aetheric construction matrix might have accidentally been re-routed to the Card House's basement."

Alex tried and failed to form a picture from Magi's description. "So some magic bullshit happened."

"No— look, I'll break it down for you. A construction matrix—"

"I'll text it to you."

"All I'm saying is that Google is free," Magi grumbled as Alex hung up.

He listened at the walls for movement in the apartment around him, but everything was quiet. He waited in the common space for confrontation, furious and craving catharsis. He found rice and instant potatoes and ate them while he waited.

When nothing continued to happen, he got cleaned up and waited some more. Someone left their room, but they passed him without saying anything. He should have been relieved, but the silence left him uncertain. Finally, he grabbed his jacket and left the house.

He walked and smoked, taking in as much of the neighborhood as he could. Besides the depots and factories that made up most of the landscape, there were a few stores. There was one old shoe store with a torn green awning, a leftover from another era, with a cast on their gate made to look like a brick wall. At the end of every workday, the clerk hooked and pulled down a rolling wall of brick and mortar that always fell out of line with the brick around it.

He bummed a swipe at the station and found himself in Manhattan, where it seemed natural to drift towards the Card House.

He saw Mika on the corner, with Sam, when he reached the building. Sam gave him a pound and a hug.

"Magi said something weird to me on the phone about needing Loisaida's number. What's going on?" Alex asked.

Sam raised an eyebrow. "You ain't heard? Whole front of a couple of buildings fell."

He gaped. "Holy shit. Is everybody all right?"

"Nobody we know got hurt."

"Where did it happen?"

"Over there," Mika said, waving down the block with her groceries. She switched her grip to reach her keys. "C'mon upstairs, we've got a great view from the roof."

MIKA STOPPED AT her apartment to put down her groceries, and from behind her, Sam reached into the bag to fish out three cans of beer. On the walk up the stairs, Mika told Alex about the house shaking as the buildings crumbled. She propped open the rooftop door with a brick and led him across the roof to look down Avenue C. On one side of the building, traffic passed as it normally did, but the other was frozen in the shadow of the three gutted buildings, lit by emergency lights.

Mika stretched a sleeve around her hand to protect it from the cold beer can. "There's a new tunnel in our basement that we all agree wasn't there last night. Magi thinks the collapse is related."

"What do you think?"

"I agree."

"Why?"

She shrugged. "Action causes reaction. Otherwise, two sudden changes in the same span of time is just a really specific coincidence. And— you know— he's not bad at this stuff."

"He's not good, though."

She shrugged again. "If you say so."

They admired the orange safety equipment against the gray rubble for a while, until the cold became too much for Alex. Shivering, he tossed his empty can across the street as hard as he could. It missed the opposite roof, bounced down the side of the building, and rolled harmlessly into the street.

"It's cold," he announced.

"You're right," Mika agreed. Sam drained her beer, crumpled the can, and chucked it. It sailed to the opposite roof and bounced twice. Satisfied, she led them down the stairwell.

Voices echoed around them, indistinct but passionate. One spoke briefly but firmly, while the other made long, shouted accusations. After two flights, the voices were clear enough to make out. Alex recognized Loisaida's clipped tones, but the rough voice yelling back was unfamiliar to him. No matter how far he tried to crane over the banister, he couldn't see any farther than the small square of yellowing linoleum between them.

"Jeez, they're still going at it," Sam muttered.

"Who is?" he asked.

She rolled her eyes. "Who else? Loisaida and Bonnie."

"How sorry can you be if you're not even gonna try and help us?" Bonnie roared.

"I am trying, but nothing can be done until I've found out where it came from," Loisaida said through gritted teeth.

"Why not?"

"Because to fix it, I need to know why it's broken, and how it was supposed to be, or I could collapse the street."

There was a brief silence. When Bonnie spoke again, she sounded as weary as Loisaida. "Why can't you cover it up?"

"I could, but that wouldn't give you any protection. That's what you want, right, protection?"

"That's exactly why I don't want to wait for tomorrow! Why can't you give us something temporary?"

"You can buy a cheap house block for this door at the hardware store."

"Ugh, the blocks there—" —the rest of the sentence was spoken too quietly to hear from the third floor until a new concern caused her voice to spike. "Do you have an idea of where this tunnel goes?"

Loisaida answered slowly. "I have an idea that it might lead to Thundertown. I negotiated for a handful of exits to be opened in my territory, and I suspect I was given a bad deal."

By this time, Sam, Mika and Alex stood on the second landing, looking down at the lobby. Bonnie and Loisaida stood apart, their arms crossed, both too engrossed to notice them eavesdropping.

Pounding feet thundered up from the basement, and Magi burst through the door. He brushed past Loisaida and Bonnie, while behind him, the sounds of footsteps continued.

Loisaida pushed Bonnie back as a twisted knot of hands and feet breached the doorframe. From the second floor, the shape looked like a wave of rotating limbs, reaching and grabbing. As Alex watched, his eyes isolated familiar shapes in the writhing mass, torsos and hips, two necks and chins, made up of the desiccated form of two human bodies. Magi climbed the second story panting, pushed his way past them, and fell into his apartment.

Loisaida appeared near the second floor, rearing up suddenly on seven feet of snake-like coils. "Start up your block!"

Above them, doors opened. People poked their heads out of their rooms, took one look at what was happening on the ground floor, and vanished. The sounds of locks bolting shut echoed through the hallway, and the burnt plastic smell of a dozen protective wards all starting at once wafted through the air. Mika scooped up Alex and shoved him through her door.

Magi was digging through one of the milk crates from the sofa, books, necklaces, and scarves scattering.

"Sheldon, start the block!" Mika shouted. Sam was still on the landing, sliding into a defensive stance as if preparing to punch the mantipede with her bare fists. Mika dragged her into the apartment, bolted the door, and reached for the ancient, cracked aluminum casing around the block on their apartment.

"No, no, don't block us in," Magi said. He took a pleather-bound notebook from the crate, untied the strap, and flipped through it like he was about to prove an argument with a dictionary. "I've got this."

Mika made a noise that was half disgust, half disbelief. Her hand stayed on the latch, as if deciding whether she should lock him in or out. Slowly, she took her hand off the block and opened the door.

On the other side, Loisaida was sidewinding up the stairs so fast the coils of muscle thundered like feet. From beneath the banister, they saw long fingers haul up a skeletal body hand over hand. Four eyes on two heads, melted scalp to scalp like plastic toys over a campfire, locked with theirs.

Then there was a sound like wood hitting wood and the thing was smacked back down to the floor. Alex looked back and saw Magi, holding his art-supply notebook open, with the dumbest look of pure joy he had ever seen.

He looked at each of them with shining eyes and teeth. *"It worked."*

"Close the damn door!" Loisaida ordered, then dove head-first over the railing, landing directly onto the creature.

There was a clanging noise above them, and one of the half-finished bikes from the fourth floor slammed into the banister before cartwheeling down to the lobby. Loisaida and the monster were temporarily tangled together before Loisaida managed to wrench the frame away and slam it down onto the spider.

Still beaming, Magi side-stepped Mika and began to climb the stairs.

Her eyes followed him with a stricken look. "Shel, please—"

"I'm gonna go get to some high ground. Wait for me inside."

She looked to Sam and Alex for support, or advice, or opinions, but Alex was lost, and Sam stood in Mika's apartment with balled fists and grinding teeth. Tom burst out of his apartment, waving a length of pipe, ran screaming to the lobby, and she gave chase, already swinging her fists.

On the ground floor, they heard Loisaida squawk. "Get away from me!"

From the banister, they could see Tom swing his pipe blindly, while Sam snatched one wriggling limb out of the air before it could hit her. The mantipede clawed at Loisaida's flesh, fingers of bone and leathery skin puncturing the soft, waxy scales. Then there was a sudden explosion like a car backfiring. Two more bursts of noise followed the first. Bonnie skidded into view, her feet pounding on the floor as she bared her teeth and pointed a gun down into the fray.

"Oh my god," Mika gasped. "Who gave you a gun?"

She didn't answer. With one hand supporting the other, she took aim, let out a long breath through her teeth, and fired. A dark splatter on the tile behind the mantipede signaled a hit. There was a guttural sound, like pipes rattling in a throat, and Loisaida slammed the mess of legs and arms against the wall. She reached into its chest and tore something away from the man-spider, something only visible for a second in the way light reflected off it, like spiderweb threads. Alex felt like his eyes refocused, like looking through a camera lens at the moment it recognized a face. The mantipede stiffened, sagged, and then slid to the floor like a puppet with cut strings.

As silence settled over the lobby, an orb of light slowly floated down through the stairwell. It bounced like a balloon against the handrails, then slowly drifted to the floor and rolled listlessly in circles. Bonnie cocked her pistol at it. Sam stepped back, Tom raised his pipe, and Loisaida slowly lifted her hands. The ball jiggled in place.

"Sorry! My bad," Magi called down. "I thought that was gonna be a fireball."

Mika recovered first and pounded down the stairs, with Alex following out of some half-understood fear that something might go wrong on her way to the lobby.

"Who's hurt?" Loisaida asked wearily as she picked her way out of the rubble on a new pair of legs.

No one answered. She went to each of them, lifting their arms and turning them around like a nurse until she was satisfied. Alex's eyes were drawn to the dried-out body of the monster. The top layer of skin parted and rolled like old paper before dissolving into powder to reveal the fragile, rough threads holding its skeleton together. Its arms and legs slid away as muscle and tissue dissolved, loosening its ribs like beads on an old necklace, shoulders collapsed around its sternum. The jaw fell, the cranium drooped, and the body curled forward, vertebrae coming loose as all the ligaments and sinews holding it together came undone. The skeletons recognizably human shapes brought him sharply to the realization that he had watched something—possibly two things— die. He felt his stomach turn over but struggled to look away.

"Did that come from Thundertown?" Sam asked.

"I'm not sure," Loisaida said.

"Did you kill it?" Alex asked.

She met his eyes. "There was nothing to kill. This is a construct built out of old bones."

Their recognizable shape was coming apart as each bone separated along its fault lines, spreading crumbs across the tile. The stale smell of ozone wafted down from above as all the blocks in the house unlatched in rapid succession. Erica, in the third closest apartment to the lobby, appeared at the head of the stairs. She froze mid-step and covered her mouth as it crumbled into a wave of dust before her.

"What happened?" she asked, gathering her skirts up delicately. Her searching gaze fell on Bonnie. "Why do you have a *gun*?"

Bonnie put the safety on and tucked it into the pocket of her hoodie with a short, defensive gesture. "Protection."

"Oh my god, from where?" Erica asked. "Oh, god. Oh, god. Is it clean? Do you have a permit? Do you even know how to use it?"

LOISAIDA LICKED HER thumb and rubbed an ash stain on the breast of her jacket, then looked down at the body, which was rapidly becoming more of a stain than an object. "This proves a point; I can't risk keeping this exit open, but I still need time. For now, put a block on this door. I'll come by to close it tomorrow."

"How do we reach you?" Bonnie asked.

Loisaida picked her purse up from the floor, took out her wallet, and removed a thin, beige card. Next, she fished out a ballpoint pen and wrote a complicated equation on the back, then drew a circle and handed the card to Bonnie.

"If any of you need to speak to me, tap there."

"I've got one for you," Alex said. She paused on her way out the door to take the Kijkaan's business card out of his hand with a short, precise nod.

Sam took a step to the side to stand in her way. She extended a hand, which Loisaida looked down at, confused. Tentatively, she reached back into her purse and put a card in Sam's hand. Sam's fingers closed around it, and she tucked it into her pocket.

The door was barely shut behind her before Sam went to it. A chill creased Alex's back.

"Wait a minute—what are you thinking?"

She gave him a look that answered his question; she was going through that door.

"No," he said. He wanted it to sound firm and powerful, the way Loisaida did when she came to a decision. Instead, it sounded petulant.

Her eyes narrowed.

"You can't," he said, still grasping for authority. "It's stupid."

Her expression made it clear that there was little he could do to stop her, although he was welcome to try. He tried to be angry, or confrontational, but couldn't find it in him. He'd done everything he could for her— if he couldn't count on her after everything he'd done, he'd done it for nothing.

"I got a way into the Tunnels and a way to contact Loisaida. It's better than I ever had," she said.

"Are you crazy? Something just came out of there. What if there's *more*?"

"How come they didn't follow this one?" she asked.

"Because— how should I know ?" he snapped, scrambling for the words to eloquently explain how stupid he found that excuse.

Fortunately, Bonnie had a reason ready. "Do you really think that cave is safe now?"

"I could check."

Bonnie snorted. "Then you're stupid *and* crazy. You really think there was only one of those things down there."

Sam said nothing.

He wanted her to be wrong; he wanted to find twenty of those monsters swarming the basement, then he wanted to go back to his mom's couch to watch Star Wars on Nails's computer. He wanted to leave this problem to the people in the house and worry instead about how he and Nails were supposed to share a couch. But Nails was gone, and Alex couldn't pretend he'd come out of the tunnels in a few days with nothing but cool stories.

"I been down there already," Sam argued.

"You got lucky! Can't be that every time," Bonnie shot back.

She unzipped her coat to show her the shield. "How 'bout this?"

"That's not reliable!"

She zipped back up with a sneer. "Well they have less. Better go rescue some people."

Chapter Twelve

AFTER THE GOLEM'S attack, Loisaida's took out the Kijkaan's card and followed the thread up to his bolthole, where she found him sitting alone in the dark, eyes shining. He was smaller and more humanoid then she expected—a gnome, perhaps.

"Evening, my Lady."

"Evening," she responded.

"What can I help you with?"

Loisaida held her anger back. It was so real she could feel it between her hands, like the reins on a bucking horse. Her nails dug into her palms. "You intentionally misinterpreted our agreement."

He sighed and parted his hands as if she was being completely unreasonable. "How could you say that?"

"How could I say that? One of the exits I negotiated for appeared in an apartment building!"

The Kijkaan didn't seem flustered or embarrassed; all he did was shrug. "The Aether has a mind of its own, Senator."

"The Aether didn't build that tunnel."

"I'm sorry the results weren't perfect, but the task was Sisyphean."

"Where was it going?"

His fingers drummed on the table. "Senator, I understand how you feel about me, and my business—"

"Where it was going?"

"—but I tried my best with the information I had. Can't that be enough?"

"No. I want our agreement settled," Loisaida snapped. "You owe me."

He held out his hands. "What was I supposed to do? Where should an exit go? We can't open them at random; the agreement was with you, so you must host them."

"But why didn't you put it in an *abandoned* building?"

"I assumed I did. The lot we found didn't have a management office attached to it."

She grit her teeth. Of course it didn't— the tenants owned the house. "Then you were aware of the golem."

He didn't respond. Even his fingers stopped their tapping.

"Why was that in there, waiting for them?"

"I don't know."

The air hung with silence. Quickly, he amended, "The security agency must have been using it."

"Why don't you know!?" she demanded. He tried to protest, apologize, explain himself, but she shouted over him. "If you hired them, you should know their methods! If you hired them, they should have known about the situation! Do you throw money at people without asking how they'd use it?"

"It could have been activated by accident when the tunnel was moved, or maybe someone left it on after construction was finished—"

"You should have been aware of those risks!" she roared, wringing her hands. "You hired a security agency that uses human remains in attack constructs to guard a *footpath*. We had an agreement, and you fucked up so badly, there was a fuck-up inside your fuck-up."

"Then I will fix it!" he shouted back, slamming his fist on the desk.

She stopped to breathe and closed her eyes, skimming her internal map of her land. Hundreds of years of change piled on top of each other, forming a kind of visual static, overlaying eras of the past. Instinct drew her to the riverbed, which always developed the slowest, even after Robert Moses put a highway along the bank—against her express desires. Now, with space limited but ambitions high, construction sites appeared like mushrooms at its base. She might be able to call a few and halt construction for a while until she could find a more permanent home for the exit.

The companies would be furious, but there wasn't much they could do, except purchase fealty from a different Lord on behalf of the whole building. She told herself that was a selfish thought to be addressed another day.

"Fine," she said. "I'll provide the space for exits. I'll have news for you by tomorrow night."

"Will this conclude our agreement? Do you find our other terms acceptable?" he asked cautiously.

"Yes," she said, trying to catch her breath.

"You'll donate your below-ground territory to the Lord Beneath?"

She raised her hand, deferring to him. "Those were our terms."

The Kijkaan's entire demeanor changed, becoming once again professional and smooth. "I'll send down the contract for your staff to read. Welcome to the board, and I want you to know that I appreciate your dedication to the community. It's a rare thing in the courts."

"Thank you."

"Not to mention the obvious resources your territory boundaries provide for us. You are sitting on one of the most impressive pieces of real estate in the City."

Loisaida opened her mouth but forgot how she wanted to respond. "That can't be true."

"I'm not a liar," he said.

"Kiernan in Williamsburg must have more space than me, and he's in hot territory these days."

The Kijkaan shook his head. "You should talk to him more often. Kiernan loses ground every day. He's always been at odds with the Horse in the north and Dibbuk in the east, and now the humans are tilting power whenever it suits their need. Their serfs have fled. They don't have the support or resources to challenge interlopers anymore."

It dawned on Loisaida how much her position had changed. Less then ten years ago, she held a reasonable chunk of land and a title given to her by a friend, but now her neighbors were being swept away in a landslide of disputes. Kiernan, the Horse and Dibbuk had been in a political cold war for decades. If they were at the point where human interference could stir them into territory disputes, then they were long past the point of reconciliation. The end of the Astors was the end of an era, but who would have guessed that her generation—who learned to negotiate with human builders to keep a controlling interest in their affairs—would fall under the weight of the tide? Who knew that Lords like Horse and Dibbuk, who rose up through popular support, would fall the same way? Through sheer dumb luck, she managed to outlast the European Lords with their legitimist claims, and the Warlords who bribed and battled their way into seats of power.

Suddenly the Kijkaan's hot-cold attitude towards her made sense.

She forced a smile. "Have you approached any of *them* with your proposal?"

"Not yet," the Kijkaan said. "But perhaps, if you were on our team, you could speak to them. I know you have a history with managing their disputes."

"True."

"You'll have the contract by tomorrow," he promised. "Tell me where you want the next two exits, and we'll settle this agreement."

He let the thread fray and the image dim, allowing Loisaida to drift back into her office. As soon as she felt settled, she flipped open her laptop and wrote out an e-mail to the daytime staff, telling them to put their current projects on hold and contact as many phase one construction sites as possible. She needed a list of sympathetic companies, and their lot numbers, immediately. She imagined the manager's face falling as she wrote it out, but they would thank her. Or they would never know what she spared them, and that was another reward.

WHEN ALEX GOT back to Staten Island, he dumped his backpack onto the couch and sorted through his belongings, packing what he needed. He shoved the rest into a trash bag, tied it shut and left it in the closet. His mother had a plastic tub full of tools above her jackets, and he took it down to see if there was anything he could use. There were a box cutter and a full package of razors, which he took. He packed more trash bags for waterproofing, remembering the smell of swamp water Sam brought back.

Now he needed to tell the mothers.

He turned on the TV and flipped through channels while his mind buzzed. They didn't have a way to leave Thundertown once they were there, but they had Loisaida's business card to call her if they needed her. They had no way to contact Nails or navigate the underground, but they did have his full name. Sam's people were still an unknown quantity, but she was too stubborn to give them up.

Lisa came home at six and went straight upstairs to change. His mother came home about thirty minutes later and fell onto the couch with a heavy sigh.

"Don't get old," she said. He pulled his face into a smile. The time was now. If he waited any longer, he wouldn't tell her.

"Mom, you remember how I said Nails was missing?"

She stopped rubbing her face and turned to look at him. The words were caught in his throat, but he felt like she could see them tangled there.

She nodded, stood, and went upstairs.

"Wait—" he said, but she ignored him and threw open her bedroom door. He could hear drawers banging open and shut, and a few minutes later, she came back down, unwrapping a tattered, flaking bundle of fabric. She laid it down on the coffee table and carefully withdrew a tiny leather box pressed with a flower relief. With her thumb, she unlatched a brass hook as small as a letter on a keyboard and gently opened it to reveal a daguerreotype in a brocade copper frame. The velvet on the opposite leaf was cut open and inlaid with smoky, warped plastic. Through the little window, he could see what looked like a prayer medallion. The picture was of a little black girl lying in a bed of flowers.

"Do you know what this is?" she asked.

He spoke quietly, "That's the girl who used to come to my window at night."

She reached out to lace her fingers in his. "She was my great-great-aunt. Her name was Lucinda Esperanza Carmen-Herrera. She died of polio when she was seven. Her brother, my great-great-grandfather, took her memorial photo and made it a genius loci— have you heard of that?"

He'd heard the word before but felt too pressured to think. "Smart... location?"

"No," she said. "What he did was use her name and her shape as a basis to define a protective ward. That's fifteen yards of protection."

Her words stunned him. A twenty-dollar block from the hardware store could maybe cover fifteen feet.

"This is the one thing from your great-grandfather's estate I wouldn't let your uncles have," she said proudly, brushing loose threads of velvet off the picture. "If they want to brag about how much richer and smarter they are then us, they can buy their own."

"This is why we don't pay the Lords," Alex said slowly.

"Right." She closed the box again. "Advocabit."

The temperature in the room dropped, and two lights ignited in a dark corner. The little black girl in white emerged. He choked on his next breath.

Natalia gave the little girl a short nod. "There she is— watching us, checking us out, seeing what we're up to. Are you OK?"

"I'm fine."

"Good. Did you catch the trigger word? Advocabit. That's important. Remember it. It's Latin. I think it means 'to summon.' It's written in the little window if you need it," Natalia said, pointing to a slip of paper sitting under the silver disk.

"I can't take that—it's the house block."

"Yes, you can. You have to. You need it. I don't need it— I don't have enemies."

Lisa appeared at the top of the stairs. Her eyes darted between them, then came to rest on Alex as she found her words. "Are you going down for him?"

"Yes."

He was struck down by how wrong the situation was. He was not the person to give priceless heirlooms to. At the same time, he couldn't explain that to either of these women, who survived too much to see this experience as more than a trial. One daguerreotype was an easier challenge than anything Natalia or Lisa had done, like getting pregnant in law school or covering ambulance shifts during a crime wave.

"This is not a request," Natalia insisted. "You *are* taking this. You're not going alone."

All three of them stared him down, the girl's eyes burning coolly from their dark corner, his mother daring him to challenge her, Lisa on the verge of tears. He made eye contact with the little girl, pristine in her dress, impossible to read behind the spotlights of her eyes. He and his mother argued about most things, like his future and how he was living his present, but in this instance, he knew she was right. He'd be safer with Lucinda.

"How do you turn her off?" he asked.

"She doesn't turn off."

He nodded and revised his question. "How do you get her to stop staring at you?"

She cracked a small smile. "You don't. Lucinda is there to mark the focal point of the shield. She understands most things to do with her job, like, for example, me giving this to you. You can talk to her, a little. Not much."

He bent down to look inside the window. In it was a small silver disk, and a strip of paper, marked with the word in neat font. Looking closer at the silver disk, he realized that the symbols on it were Hebrew.

"What's the disk say?" he asked.

"I don't know. It was written by the designer," she said. She closed the daguerreotype, wiped off the paper crumbs and gently folded the box back into its soft cocoon. He added a layer of plastic before zipping it up as carefully as he could into his backpack. Natalia gave his hand a firm squeeze.

"And one more warning; don't think you're invincible, now. That's how people get hurt."

With that, the conversation was over. Natalia sat back down on the couch to channel-surf, but quickly snapped off the box, and went to her room. From the living room, he heard a rumble across the floor, as if someone was moving the furniture. Twice he got up and unraveled the bundle of fabric swaddling, to check on the picture.

Lisa came downstairs and held him tight, pressing something into his hand.

"I don't have anything else," she said. "Take care of Dave."

She pushed away and ran back upstairs. When he opened his hand, he found a roll of twenties, which he put into the heel of his boot.

"YOU'RE NOT FUCKING walking into that tunnel, Sam," Bonnie said the next day, toe tapping against the floor. Sam ignored her and went for the basement door, but found it locked.

Bonnie smiled. "Nobody's coming in or out before Loisaida gets here."

Sam glanced back at Alex, fidgeting with the zipper on his coat. "Guess we wait for Loisaida."

"Yes, we are!" Bonnie sputtered furiously. She stormed towards the stairs, turned, stormed back, and kicked a loose tile across the floor. "Fuck! You're not a kid anymore, how could you still act so stupid? You should be home right now. Go home. Go home!"

They stood chest to chest, Bonnie staring into Sam's face, while she looked over Bonnie's head to the staircase beyond.

"You think you're so goddamn tough, but guess what, so does everybody else. Everybody thinks they're so goddamn tough until somebody tougher comes along. When you go down there, you have to be ready for every macho piece of shit that wants to prove something— every single fucking one."

Sam's lips were pressed tightly together, a controlled kind of rage burning below the surface. Slowly, she said, "That's your reason to leave people there?"

"People? Who? What people?" Bonnie asked. "The only person I know is you, and I'm doing what I can to keep you from making bad decisions."

"Thanks, Mom," Sam said, without a hint of emotion. She stared straight back at Bonnie as if waiting for her to make the first move.

"You're welcome," Bonnie answered, without irony. They stared each other down for a long time, waiting for the other one to blink. Alex became acutely aware of the passage of time, ticking down the minutes until the sun set and Loisaida arrived. "Are we doing this, or what?"

"We're doing this. We're waiting right here for Loisaida," Bonnie said. Sam said nothing. Agitated, she added, "She's going to agree with me. You're not getting in."

No response.

"Fucking kids."

"I already been down there," Sam said, at last.

"God bless," Bonnie answered, throwing up her hands. "Now you want to go back there to test your luck again."

Sam looked over at Alex. "Let's wait upstairs."

She squeezed past Bonnie and climbed the stairs, following Alex into Magi and Mika's apartment.

"Wait all you want," Bonnie snapped and went back to pacing.

The door was unlocked, and Magi looked up from his place on the makeshift couch, bare feet propped up to expose dust-coated soles with stray notes of glitter. The space heater hummed and rotated before him. The heat was out again, either because of the hole in the basement or for any of the other problems in the half-constructed old building. He blinked with mild surprise at the sight of Sam and Alex. "Hello. What are you doing here?"

"Hiding from Bonnie," Mika said for them.

Magi's expression remained blank. "Oh— why?"

"Because she's a lunatic," she answered dryly.

His expression did not clear. "I don't think she's a lunatic."

Mika rolled her eyes.

"We're gonna go down into that Tunnel," Sam told him, taking a seat opposite Mika at the card table under the window.

His whole face lit up. "Can I come?"

Sam shrugged.

"Shel— no— wait a minute— are you serious?" Mika cried.

"Yes?" he said, blinking curiously at her. "I want to see what Thundertown is like, maybe pick up some Aether designs and try a few out."

"You can't come with us if you're coming to bend reality," Alex interjected.

He made a face. "I need to practice."

"You can practice here," Mika said, fingers curling into her coat.

"I have been. But I want to do something bigger."

Her face fell. "Shel, that cave could fall down on your head at any time."

Magi stopped to consider her argument, then frowned. "I still want to go. Anyway, I'll be with these two, I'll be fine."

"What are they going to do if there's a cave-in?" she demanded.

He shrugged. "Three's safer than one."

"Three's—" She slapped the card table. "What the fuck is *wrong* with you!??"

"She's right," Alex piped up.

Magi looked up from where he was taking things out of a milk crate and shoving them into a bag, blinking rapidly. "There was a cave-in above ground yesterday."

No one answered.

His blinking slowed. "I want to go."

Mika unlatched the door and stepped out without a word. With a sigh, Magi lifted two other milk crates and started to sort them.

Alex followed Mika out. He found her sitting on the stairs with her head in her hands. She made a sign for him to approach, tucking in her skirt to make space between her and the wall for him.

"Thanks for checking up on me."

"Don't worry about it."

She chewed her lip, digesting her thoughts. "You get why I'm upset, right?"

He nodded.

"Do you think I'm crazy?"

He shook his head.

She sighed and put her head down. "I mean, he's your friend. You probably agree with him."

"He's my friend, but no, I do not. I have to go down there. Nails is missing."

She peeked through her fingers to smile at him. "I feel crazy. I keep picturing all the ways it can go wrong, but he acts like it's impossible. Even if there's nothing dangerous down there, what would any of you do if one of you tripped on an ordinary rock and twisted your ankle? If I brought this up, he'd say—"

She did an accurate impression of Magi's thousand-mile stare and mimicked his voice. "'Well, actually, people live down there, so the roads probably aren't that dangerous.'" She dropped the impression and slumped her shoulders. "But he's never been there before. Why would anyone want to go spelunking without spelunking gear, anyway?"

Alex didn't have an answer. Every minute they didn't spend in the tunnel was another minute he spent second-guessing his decision.

Sam and Magi stepped out of the apartment. She caught their eyes and pointed down the stairs with a quizzical tilt of her head. Alex rose, leaving Mika on the stairs, and got his bag out of the living room.

Bonnie stopped her pacing when she saw them at the top of the stairs and watched them descend with a blazing expression.

"No," she said, blocking the door. "No! You're not going!"

"Yes, we are," Sam said.

"No!"

"I guess we can wait back upstairs," Magi suggested.

"*You're not going!*" she shouted as they climbed back to Mika's apartment.

There, they found her packing. She refused eye contact. "So, what, you guys think you can take a troll, but you can't handle one crazy old lady?"

She shut the bag with an angry zip and went upstairs to knock on Erica's door.

"Can I borrow the key to the basement?" she asked when Erica answered the door.

Erica looked at her, Alex, Sam and Magi, then took a key down from a hook somewhere behind her door. "Going down to Thundertown, huh?"

"Yes, ma'am."

"I better come distract the dragon," she muttered, closing her door behind her.

Bonnie greeted them on the ground floor with shock and horror. "What the hell are you doing, E? Are you on their side?"

"I came down to find out why you've been yelling at people all day," Erica said, passing the keys to Mika behind her back.

"These stupid kids are trying to get themselves killed, walking into a Thundertown with no protection."

"Bonnie, squatting this building could have got us killed."

"Oh, please, this is not the same."

Meanwhile, Mika snuck behind them and tried the key in the lock.

"Don't you dare!" Bonnie screamed, grabbing her wrist. Mika struggled, panicked, and pushed back.

Erica tried to separate them. "Everybody calm down! We're not about to start a brawl over a door!"

"She opened it!" Bonnie frothed, shaking Mika. "She can't open it! Loisaida said not to!"

Erica pulled with all her might to pry her off Mika. "Bonnie, calm down—"

"No!" She threw her whole weight forward, bringing Erica with her. She fell face-first into the door. Sam grabbed Bonnie by the armpits and hoisted her up like a doll, where she swung bonelessly.

"No! No! No! No! You can't! You can't!"

Sam pushed her off and stepped through the frame.

"No!"

Alex squeezed in behind her.

"You can't!"

Magi and Mika quickly followed. Still howling, Bonnie threw open the door and chased after them, kicking and yelling as they walked into the tunnel. They were two yards into the white rock before she finally stopped. They were still within sight of the basement when she bolted back up the stairs.

"Lights," Sam said, and three flashlights lit up the cave. As they walked, she glanced over her shoulder and smiled. "She gets that way."

"How do you know her?" Alex asked.

"I used to live here for a while."

Alex was surprised. "When?"

"In middle school, and a little bit in high school. They were nice. More runaways around, back then."

A new light from behind them proceeded the slapping of boots on the stone. They backed against the wall, huddled together, but instead of another mantipede, Bonnie came into view, zipping up a coat and bag.

"You'd all die without me," she swore.

Chapter Thirteen

NAILS STRUGGLED TO remember if this was his dream or reality as he floated through the darkness. Too soon, someone came to wake him. He groaned and rolled away, determined to stay in bed, but they were persistent. When he cracked his eye open, he found himself in his room at his grandparents' house in Westchester, the walls still pastel-blue for a toddler, the shelf over his dresser full of toys he never played with.

"Go ask your grampa if he can help me," his grandmother's voice said sweetly. He buried his nose into his pillow. His grandmother married her second husband late in her life, when David was ten. He never managed to warm up to the man, position of grandfather already filled by his father's father.

"Why can't you do it?"

"He'll think it's sweet if you do it."

He burrowed deeper, looking to hide. She played this game constantly. The one thing he didn't miss about living with his grandparents was their habit of making him stop everything to do something cutesy.

"OK, Gramma, I'll go in a second—"

"Now, David." the voice said, still exactly like his grandmother, but still different, as if taken from a memory at some other point. Frustrated, he threw back his covers and stormed out, but when he opened his door, he found his parents' apartment on the other side. His grandparents were gone.

The Kijkaan stood in the middle of his living room, reading the titles of his parents' record collection with his hands clasped behind his back.

Nails tried to blink, to clear the last shadows of sleep from his eyes. His lids were too heavy to lift, and no matter how hard he tried to focus on the Kijkaan, the harder it was.

"What are you doing in here?" He mumbled. Even speaking was hard. He felt like his mouth was closed.

The Kijkaan turned to him at last, his expression nonchalant. "I wanted to talk."

Nails scrambled to organize his thoughts, but nothing would stay in the muddy soup of his subconscious. "Fuck. Am I asleep again? Why do we have to talk like this?"

"How else?"

"By phone," he suggested. He wanted it to sound angrier, but he was too tired.

"You don't have electricity."

Nails was shocked. He tried to reach into his pocket to check his phone but struggled to find it.

"I can speak to you while you're awake if you like," the Kijkaan offered. "Have you ever played Bloody Mary?"

"I seen it on tv."

"You don't need to have the lights off, but make sure you're alone. The image doesn't transmit to everyone, so a bystander might think you're talking to yourself."

He awoke with a start, still against the wall near the hotdog cart while the market continued around him. He couldn't tell if he'd only been asleep for a few minutes or an entire day.

He sat up and brushed dirt and scraps of paper off his back. The last time he lay down on the bare earth and took a nap must have been when he was a child. Slowly, he pushed himself up, moving joints gone stiff from laying on cold, hard ground. He felt his pockets, making sure he had everything still on him.

He walked the perimeter of the market. There wasn't as much to see as there was at the larger one in the old Thundertown, although people seemed as surprised to see him. It was like a flea market fused with a farmer's market, with racks of fresh meat next to piles of batteries and corny porcelain figurines sitting in nests of tangled wall chargers. There were long johns and T-shirts, shoes, handbags, dried herbs, live animals and people who didn't have stands, who carried their wares in bags, or pushed them in carts, spitting a spiel whenever they made eye contact. Musicians were playing for tips, and stereos blasting all kinds of music.

He had a few dollars and some small things in his pocket he'd be happy to sell for food or water. As he was counting them up, he noticed a twelve-year-old girl walking confidently through the market.

She had brown skin and long black hair tied back into a tight bun; she wore a dirty pink jacket with a mud-streaked backpack. He studied her for a sign that she was anything but a young girl, but nothing about her casual, brisk pace revealed anything, beyond a clear destination ahead. In documentaries, Folk lures looked like cheap, plastic copies, but he always heard that in the wild, laden with illusions, adrenaline made them real.

He watched her curiously as she wandered around the market.

Nails's attention fell to a hand-lettered sign propped up against an overflowing shopping cart, which said CHARGING STATION, $5 PER DEVICE. A small man in a fringed jacket leaned nearby. As he got closer, he saw the cart was full of military surplus and camping gear.

The man gave him a winning smile as he approached. "Charge your devices? Takes me three seconds, no exaggeration."

"Sold." He handed the man his phone.

When he cracked his knuckles, white sparks popped from the joints. His hands began to glow until the shadow of his bones appeared through the meat of his hands. Heat and static filled the air around him, lifting stray threads of his hair.

As soon as it started, it was over. The air cooled, his skin dulled, and when he opened his hands, the plastic casing on the phone sat solid and undisturbed in his palm.

Nails wordlessly took his property out of the man's radioactive hands and buried it deep in his pocket.

"Want me to do anything else?"

"No, but I want that."

"Which?" He looked down. "Oh, that. Vietnam-style frame pack in olive drab. All-Purpose Lightweight Individual Carrying Equipment, or ALICE to her friends. It's not a real relic, it's made out of some weird plastic material. I'll give it to you for twenty, it's been repaired."

He turned it over to show Nails the stitches on the adjustment straps.

"Twenty? C'mon, man, you already said it's not real, and it's been repaired. I'm taking it off your hands. Cut me a deal."

"It's like I says it is. And the bag is fifteen dollars."

"How much would you pay for it?"

"Fine— twelve, and one of those patches you've got on."

Nails looked down at his jacket. The ones he was wearing weren't coming out easily, but he was sure he had extras stashed somewhere. After patting himself down, he found three buttoned in a side pocket and spread them like cards. "Deal."

The man looked over the patches in his hands one by one, then picked the coolest one, an embroidered patch in a military style with a sword. It was worth more then the difference he'd talked him down from. He let his heart sink as the man rubbed his thumb over the stitches, then picked up the ALICE pack, trying to take assurance in the way the frame dug into his shoulders.

He went around the market one more time, looking for something to put in his new pack. He drifted away from the stalls, crunching through broken glass littered around piles of trash growing in corners of the market.

He spotted another human walking towards an exit and followed him. Like the girl, the man made eye contact with no one, keeping his head up and his hands in his pockets. His coat was an interesting patchwork of leather, hide and fur, and his shoes were giant, plastic Mickey Mouse boots, like a sewage worker's. Something about his swagger made the clothes look borrowed.

The tunnel connected to another corner of the market, where the man broke through the crowd and made a beeline for a small group of humans sitting together on a collection of old park furniture. Chairs, chess tables, and benches were thrown together in a jumbled clump, some upside-down, some broken. The man picked a rusty iron-wrought chair and plopped down next to a black woman with grown-in braids and an MTA conductor's uniform, who was fitting a 75 lumens bulb into a giant red lantern. The little girl in the pink coat was talking while the woman nodded periodically.

Hesitantly, he walked toward them. They all watched him approach, measuring him up.

"Hi," he said. He put down his bag in front of him and smiled, hands in front of him to prove they were empty. "I'm Dave."

"Are you lost?" the black woman asked.

"Yes, ma'am," he said. "I got into a fight upstairs and got sent down here to think about what I'd done."

The man with the leather-hide coat laughed. "That's a new one."

She gave the man a reproachful look before turning back to Nails. "I'm Cassandra."

The man reached forward to shake his hand. "My name's Rich. New down here?"

"Can't you tell?"

Cassandra made a tone of disapproval.

"What?" Rich asked. "The more, the merrier. Misery loves company."

A round black man spoke up. "Did anyone hear about another exit?"

A redhead Hasid answered. "Everyone says all the exits were closed after 9/11."

The woman with the lantern shook her head. "They've been taking surveys on all the Thundertowns since the '60s. There's no way they wrapped it up right after 9/11."

"Yeah, something's got to be open," a light-skinned man with salt and pepper stubble added.

"Otherwise, we wouldn't be here," the round black man agreed.

Rich scoffed. "If they're here, but we can't find them, then they might as well be closed."

Cassandra closed the window on the lantern and tested the light on the floor.

"I got another card for that guy," he continued, flicking it between his fingers. "Kidg-cahn, or however you pronounce it."

"I met that guy," Nails said, eager to help. "I don't trust him."

"Well, of course not, he has an agenda, I think we can all agree on that, but if his agenda benefits us—" Rich let the suggestion hang.

"I want to hear why he doesn't trust him," Cassandra said.

He felt awkward. His face split instinctively into a smile. "He put me in a burlap sack and kept me locked in his office."

"Did he make you spin straw into gold, too?" Rich asked.

"This is like when you tried to get us all to pay that guy at the Minetta Street exit five hundred bucks each," Cassandra muttered.

"I didn't say that, I know there's only one ATM down here. All I said was his perspective makes sense—"

The round black man picked his way through the park benches to shake Nails's hand. "What's your name?"

"Dave," he said, but changed his mind as soon as he said it. He would be traveling with this group long enough for someone to notice he didn't respond to his birth name anymore. "Nails."

"Dave Nails, all right. My name's Horace. Come in."

He stepped over the ring of broken park benches and entered the circle. The market was feet away but completely separate from them. People didn't look at them or even pass by. As time passed, the surface tension of the group broke, splitting them into smaller groups that gathered around sleeping bags and food. The man in the hide coat latched onto Nails and pulled him into his group, where the black man and the little girl in pink were struggling to make a fire.

"Let's try names again," the man said, pointing to himself. "Rich." He pointed to the girl. "Leticia." He indicated the round man. "Horace."

"Nice to meet you," Nails said, wondering what was familiar about them.

"Guys, this is Dave—"

"Dave Fingernails," Horace added.

Rich's eyebrows raised. "Uh, well, sure, I'll call you whatever you want. So guys, did you hear Dave Fingernails was sent down here after a fight?"

"That's a new one," Horace muttered, echoing Rich.

"We were on a train," Leticia said.

"A train?" Nails repeated, still smiling but only because he forgot to move his face. "That happened to a friend of mine. I think it took the whole car."

"It did," Horace said.

He was still smiling. "Do you guys know a Sam? Short for Samantha? Big girl, blonde, hardc— I mean, wears band T-shirts?"

They stared at him. Rich threw back his head and laughed.

"Cassandra!" he shouted. "This guy knows Sam! What are the odds?"

"Is Sam OK?" Horace asked.

"She's looking for all of youse guyses."

Cassandra jumped over park benches to reach them. "What's going on? You know Sam? Is she OK!??"

"Yeah, she's fine, she's back upstairs. This is great! We've been trying to find you guys since she came back, but she doesn't have any of youse guyses full names, but she has mine, so when they come looking for me—"

"Slow down. What happened to her? We were attacked," Cassandra insisted.

Nails slowed down as best as he could and filled in the story as he understood it. From their perspective, an enormous hand crawled fingers-first through a tunnel and wrapped itself around Sam before quietly, steadily drawing back.

"But she was fine! She was being saved by a giant!" Nails said.

"Why didn't that happen to the rest of us?" Cassandra asked.

"It's just that it's as hard to find help above ground as it is below. I mean, it's not like you're not looking for exits," Nails stuttered. His words comforted no one. He felt a flash of fear. He didn't want to travel alone again, and he didn't have much to offer. If they decided they didn't like him, he'd have to walk alone.

He walked back into the connecting tunnel between caverns. He took out his phone. The screen was black, empty, and reflective.

"Kijkaan," he said, and felt a sharp sting between his eyes. He blinked to clear them, but the edges stayed soft and fuzzy. "Kijkaan—"

"Once was enough," the Kijkaan said, appearing in Nails's reflection. He took in Nails's surroundings with the same polite blankness he used in his childhood home. "Are you underground?"

"Yup," he said. "Got attacked by a shapeshifter."

"I'm sorry."

"Oh, yeah, it's fine. This is your job, right? You can get me out of this, right?"

"Maybe. Possibly. I'm not sure. I spoke to Loisaida, and she requested I build an entrance to the new Thundertown. I'm not sure if you'll be able to find it."

"You'll kill a lot of birds with this stone. I connected with a group of humans, so if we can get out of here through you, you can take the whole credit."

The Kijkaan gave him the first genuine smile he'd seen, although it was sardonic and annoyed. "Well, that's certainly true."

The Kijkaan gave him instructions on how to reach the exit. The directions were meaningless, but after finding a pen in his pocket and a leftover flyer, he wrote down as much of it as he could understand and brought it back to the group. "Hey, guys, somebody from down here gave me directions to a new tunnel entrance downtown."

"Let me guess, you can lead us right there," Cassandra grumbled.

He felt a sting of self-consciousness. He pulled the flyer he'd written on out of his pocket and shoved it at her. "Here, you take it."

She did, gingerly. "We already decided while you were gone that we were going to see the Kijkaan before we did anything. You can go to the new tunnel by yourself."

As the fire burned, the group coalesced once again around it and Nails found himself outside of the circle, watching people shop at the market. It wasn't endless; people packed up and left, and while others came to replace them, as the hours stretched fewer people came. Small silhouettes gathered around the edges of their camp, but the group ate, talked, and napped, ignoring it. Nails let himself relax a little, safe enough for the moment. He bought beer from a seller and passed it around the camp.

Two green arrows glowed on the watch on Horace's wrist. Nails noticed people asked him frequently for the time, even as the hours rolled past without change. He wondered if days and weeks could pass without them noticing it, and his stomach turned sour. Sick with anxiety, he rolled over and curled up on his side to sleep it off, but the ground wasn't as comfortable or forgiving as it was when he was exhausted. He eventually found a chunk of cardboard to put between himself and the ground, and someone at a stall gave him a blanket out of pity.

He held his pounding heart in his chest and tried to tell himself he'd survived worse. There was a plan to pull them all out of this situation. Hopefully, in the morning they'd arrive in a familiar place. Hopefully they weren't going to leave the Tunnels and find that New York had advanced hundreds of years in the future.

He fell asleep uneasily, listening to the rise and fall of voices around the dying campfire.

LOISAIDA SLEPT IN her office for a handful of hours, woke up in the middle of the day and scramble down to the Card House before anything new could crawl out of the basement. The shrill white woman in her faded black hoodie was, thankfully, absent. Loisaida was greeted instead by a thin black woman in a long, flowing skirt. She led Loisaida down to the basement and asked a few gentle questions, some for herself, some for the house.

Answering her was a pleasure compared to her neighbor, and Loisaida found herself eager to explain what she was doing as she worked. The woman watched her build and weave the design, and while she watched, Loisaida talked. She explained how she allowed for the two different locations of each side of the tunnel.

"The difference between human engineers and trasgo is the way they interact with the Aether," she explained as she tied off the first half of the spell. "Humans have no awareness of the way the Aether interacts with the world, so they need to guess. Most work on a negative volume theory, by adding the mass and volume of everything they are building around and inferring a quantity from that. If I were human, I would need to measure this cave. Instead, I can see what I'm doing."

"Fascinating," the woman said. Loisaida activated the design with a sharp tug, and a white wall filled the mouth of the cavern, exactly like the walls on either side of it. The second design was much more complicated; she weaved and gestured as each portion of the design activated, drawing the tunnel back to its original location and replacing the solid rock behind it, while severing the design holding it together. She found a clause in the old design that moved existing structures out of the way in the middle of the job and re-wrote her design as it unfolded to account for basements unceremoniously shoved aside. It didn't surprise her that three buildings collapsed.

To the outside, human perspective, Loisaida seemed to be conducting a silent, invisible orchestra.

"Magi would be entranced," Erica said, finger on her lip.

"Who?"

"The other black person in the house. The one with the little journal."

"Oh— him," she said. Her hand gestures slowed down but grew broader. With huge swings of her hand, she brought the orchestra to its climax. "Is he in school for Aether Design?"

"No, his parents won't let him."

"Shame," she muttered, tying off the end.

"You haven't heard from them at all, have you?"

"Who?"

Erica turned away from her with a small, private smile. "I knew they wouldn't call you. Bonnie, Sam, Alex, Magi, and Mika all went down there before you could close the hole."

"What?" she shouted. "Why didn't you tell me?"

"They told me not to," she said simply.

Before she left, Loisaida took the golem's remains, filling her bag with its charcoal bones and chunks of skin as dry as resin. She shook everything out on her desk and raked her fingers through to gather up pinches of ash, leaving long grey streaks across her blonde wood desk, and shoved everything she could hold into manila envelopes, which she mailed to Superintendent Tal down at One Police Plaza.

That night there was an e-mail in her inbox from the office manager with the addresses of four construction companies in her territory and a package wrapped in brown paper from the Kijkaan.

The contract was as thick as a textbook and bound in plain, heavy paper. The first ten pages described the document and introduced the reader to the Lord Beneath. By entering into the agreement, Loisaida had access to the Lord's territory, resources, and serfs, as well as an alliance with all other members of the board.

The next ten pages detailed how much she could discuss with people outside of the council. Using friendly language, the document made it clear that the public had access to exactly nothing. In order to protect other members of the board from backlash, the Lord needed to be treated like a real, breathing being. They were each encouraged to share the work they were doing, so long as they remembered to act like they were working in conjunction with a separate entity. The document held no clues of an ulterior motive. The contract read as the Kijkaan described it; a dense, but thorough legal document, describing a land trust between Lords under a pseudonym. The wording was extremely generous to the trustee, instead of the collective trust, and Loisaida was briefly annoyed that her instinctive distrust wasn't rewarded with easy proof. Instead, the Lord Beneath made perfect sense; the courts were corrupt. They were built for Old World Lords to be a country club for the disgraced relatives of successful clan leaders.

As the years passed, the Court Lords had to argue amongst themselves over who had a more legitimate claim on their territory, and quickly people noticed that the court was made up of youngest sons and disinherited cousins, sent overseas specifically to get them out of the way. Some legitimists managed to keep land, but became Lords in name only, enjoying no privilege but access to a court system that didn't hold any power.

The last big push for change came in 1908 when a group of community-supported Petty Lords— Loisaida among them— occupied the downtown court building. She remembered the rush of success, the waiting crystallizing into action, the dawn of a new era. They had the chance to make a judicial court that was available to everyone, no matter who they were or where they were from.

For a short while, the new laws felt egalitarian. Anyone could become Lord. As districts adjusted to fit the boundaries of territories, it could have been easier for residents to access the courts and petition their Lords. With direct access to their residents, Lords could better work with the City. But, the same territory disputes once found in the street simply moved to the court. Lords like the King of Battle Row still spent all their time either bragging about old fights or brawling outside their favorite bars. Now people could hold a title for years without stepping foot into the court building, not because they couldn't but because they didn't want to go, and the same old problem of underrepresented populations being held hostage by indifferent Lords came again.

A cooperative like the Lord Beneath was the start of something new, but it needed to be held accountable to avoid the mistakes the courts were already repeating.

THE NEXT EVENING, Chief Tal called.

"Can I ask what's inside the ten manila envelopes you sent me?" he asked with extreme, hesitant politeness.

"I sent you the remains of a golem that climbed into an apartment in my territory. I'd just like to make sure it wasn't built from a murder victim."

"I can't use police equipment for the Night Court," Tal said, dropping his voice to a furious whisper.

"This isn't for the Night Court," Loisaida insisted.

"Loisaida-" he began.

She cut him off. "Tal, the bones were sent to you out of respect for your department. Don't you want to check to see if the bodies are from a homicide?"

"Not good enough," Tal said. "It's not a question of morals or politics, it's personal interest. Even if no other Lord finds out about the favors I'm doing for you, my superiors could find out, and they want to maintain court neutrality, too. I could lose my job."

"You have my protection," Loisaida promised.

He groaned. "Did you really send me these remains without any interests of your own?"

"I *would* like to find out where they're from," she admitted.

He put his phone on the desk to groan and curse at an arm's distance but came back a few minutes later. "Promise me this isn't going back into the New York Courts."

"I promise."

"And you better come back to pick him up," Tal added. "I'm not making my desk his final resting place."

BETWEEN PROJECTS, SHE ran over her conversation with the Kijkaan. He told her her peers were being undone by fighting, and when she searched for them, thousands of results appeared.

Humans liked nothing better than to watch trasgo fight, enough to risk their lives for it. They dove out of cover to catch footage of a bolt of lightning cutting across a clear blue sky. There was a sea of duel videos full of blurry, shaking footage, streaks of blinding light, and sprays of rubble. Plenty took place in New York, mostly around tourist-heavy spots where cameras were already out when a fight started. She found videos of the King of Battle Row performing for the crowd, circling his opponent, preening like a pigeon. In the next moment, he buried the white-hot blade of his hand into his opponents' neck, to screams from the crowd.

But there were less gruesome videos, less popular shots of the Broadway Mayor looking awkward and tired, footage of a tourist pestering the Text King, and even a few videos of a Petty Lord she didn't recognize called 'the High Queen of Bowling Green,' who seemed to spend most of her time headbutting tourists. Through it all, she found nothing to prove that humans were manipulating these interactions for any purposes higher than their follower count.

When the sun began to rise and the sky lightened from nighttime purple to a translucent blue, she was as ignorant as ever, but hours later, her office manager woke her in the middle of the day.

"What is it? What's going on?" she mumbled, still half-asleep and deeply annoyed. "Is this an emergency?"

"Yes," the manager said. "The construction company called. Their site collapsed and fell into the river."

She groaned and rubbed her eye, still too tired to understand. "Is it my responsibility?"

"Yes."

She sighed. For all the complaints she made about her staff making simple mistakes, she appreciated their honesty. "OK. I'm coming in."

She checked the time and comforted herself with the knowledge that it was not the earliest call she'd ever gotten. She prepared for the next few hours and was out the door in twenty minutes. She called the office to confirm the details of the event in the cab. A police cordon forced her to get out and walk long before they reached the site.

Sunshine reflecting off the bone-white sidewalk forced her to retreat farther below the overpass, where the thin shadows provided a blessed relief from the burning sun. The riverbed buzzed with activity as crowds of people swarmed the orange safety barriers. She pushed her way to the front and tried to flag down a cop, but they ignored her. She pushed a little more to open the barrier— and suddenly, she was surrounded by cops.

She quickly dropped her glamour, reared up, and shouted with imperious disdain, "I am Representative Loisaida."

Two cops took their hats off, while a third said, "We're very sorry, my Lady, but we need to keep everyone out of the scene."

Loisaida paused to come up with some grand and flowery language to justify her presence, but necessity won over theatrics. "The company that owns this plot called to have me investigate."

The cop shrugged. "Look, we need to keep this area clear."

"I'm not stopping you from doing *your* job." Loisaida snapped.

He smiled the smile of a public servant about to deliberately misunderstand a statement. "I appreciate you, Miss Senator. Now, if you just take a step back behind the caution tape, you'll be really helping me out."

She could see there was no point in being stubborn at someone who could be stubborn right back. "I want to see a sergeant."

On her request, an officer escorted her to the impromptu command center, where three sergeants in white shirts were listening to a dispatch on a single radio. The officer left her in the truck bed to wait.

After another few minutes, one of the white shirts finally met Loisaida's eyes. "Can I help you?"

"I need access to the site," she said.

"Can't do it," the officer said. "We need the area clear, and we can't show partiality towards the Folk."

Loisaida stuck out her jaw. "I have just as much of a right to the site as you," she said stubbornly. "I have jurisdiction over the area, and the site management specifically called for me."

"I have no way of knowing if that's true, ma'am," the sergeant said, looking over her rather then at her.

"Call them," she suggested. Before he could make more excuses, she took out her phone, but without their number, she had to call her office first, and in the interim, the cops gently guided her out of the command center and back behind the barrier.

She stood there quietly while her office manager patched her through to the company manager, who called the owner, who was on-site. Soon after she hung up the phone, a man in a button-up shirt and no coat stormed over. He was red-faced and shaking with rage.

"This is all *your* fault," he snarled. "People could have died— some people got hurt! The whole overpass nearly collapsed, and it's *your* job to fix it!"

He grabbed her by the wrist and dragged her out of the crowd.

She was in.

"Can you tell me what happened?" she asked.

He looked down at her with hate, teeth clenched in a grimace. He squeezed her wrist with all of his strength to hurt her and she, annoyed, pulled her hand away. His hand grasped the air impotently, and for a moment she thought he might take a swing at her.

Instead, he turned abruptly towards the river. "Look! You can see for yourself!"

An entire chunk of land under the highway was gone. The concrete was broken as if by a giant set of teeth, and the dirt beneath it turned to mud against the waves.

She took in the sight of the new cliff face and felt overwhelmed by the work ahead. "If you want me to fix this, you need to give me a better description of what you saw."

"How?"

"Tell me what happened."

His lips peeled back from his clenched teeth. He spoke in a slow, measured voice. "If you reattach that chunk of land, would our claim on it still hold?"

"Yes. I don't think anyone would try to challenge you on it, but if they do, I promise to act as a material witness."

His shoulders dropped a notch. "And the equipment we lost?"

She hesitated. It would be hard enough to pull up enough stone and mud to fix the ragged side of the island, without the additional complication of fishing out construction equipment. "Send me a list of missing equipment. I can't promise I can restore them, but I'll try my best."

He thought it over. She wondered what would happen if he decided to forgo discussions and move immediately into a lawsuit, but he nodded. "OK."

She relaxed. "Start by telling me what happened."

"We got a call saying there was a huge crack in the sidewalk around our property. Concrete was sticking up out of the ground. We came down here to check it out and our site fell into the East River, right in front of us."

She couldn't think of anything to say— she could barely imagine what it was like to watch the solid ground tear away. All she could think to do was fill the silence. "I'm glad there were no casualties—"

"—yet," he added, with a critical glare. "Homeless people sleep on site all the time."

Again, she didn't have an answer for him. "All I can do is try to get back as much as I can."

She left him to explore the site, ignoring the stares of first responders. She ducked the yellow tape and walked to the very edge of the disaster site. Out on the horizon was the grey blur of sky and water, dotted with a few brisk sailboats. Below her were uneven layers of stone, dirt, and torn roots hanging out of the mud like veins. The river churned and foamed at the base, and breaking the surface was one huge steel claw, and an irregular semicircle of broken concrete.

One of the three white shirts from earlier approached, waving. His hair and skin were both the same boiled orange color. "Are you our Lady?"

She nodded.

He shook her hand. "It's nice to meet you, my lady. My name is Sergeant Jones. Ask if you have any questions."

"Thank you."

"Do you mind if I ask you what your title is? The lands around here got funny boundaries."

"It's fine," she said. She could hear enough of Long Island in his accent to guess he wasn't familiar with the City. "It's Senator Loisaida."

"Senator?"

"That's right."

He bit his tongue, trying not to smile "If you don't mind me asking, how do you become a senator? Do you hold a vote or something?"

"I did, actually."

He sounded amused. "Who'd you run against? Did you have a campaign?"

"I ran against Little Syria."

"Never heard of him."

"You weren't alive when he was Lord," Loisaida said. "This all used to be his."

The cop gave Loisaida a look she'd grown used to seeing in human faces, one full of the discomfort of facing their own mortality. She wondered what the neighborhood looked like through his eyes; what did the mixture of architecture styles tell him about her home? What was it like to have no memories of a time before? She still sometimes saw the faces of friends long dead in the crowd or thought she caught a glimpse of Al-Harran, Little Syria, making his rounds through the area, visiting businesses and neighbors that didn't exist anymore. She learned everything from Al-Hassan, but he, like all teachers, could not teach her how to best use her lessons. They both agreed that the methods he'd used up to that point couldn't continue forever, and in order to force the courts to accept change, they needed someone who understood what needed to be done. Al-Hassan chose years ago to make his last act as Little Syria holding an election, as a deliberate attack on the legitimacy politics in the courts. His candidate needed to be picked carefully. His protégé needed to have legitimate lineage to protect their claim. This was a time when the term 'Petty Lord' was a peer without title or land, who orbited and often socialized within the court despite having nothing to their name. Al-Hassan could have chosen any of them, but in the end, he settled on Loisaida, an orphan with a claim on a small pocket of territory in a country she had never seen.

How strange, to look at a deli or empty office building and not have a hundred memories for it.

"Crazy," the cop said finally. "How'd he get the name? Did a bunch of Syrians used to live around here, or something?"

She didn't have the patience or the energy to give him a history lesson. "So, the site."

"The site," he agreed. "Around noon someone in parks contacted the owners saying they noticed a weird crack, or bump or something, and by the time they said they arrived at around one or one thirty, the whole thing comes falling down. Fortunately, there was no one on-site that day because you called ahead of time to warn them."

He checked her for a reaction. She gave him none.

The cop didn't waste a moment, moving smoothly on to the next part. "The freeway didn't fall, either, so no one driving by was hurt. A neighbor called us, the owners say they called you, and now we're here."

"We are."

"Care to tell us what you know?" he asked.

"I tried to have an organizer in Thundertown make public exits to evacuate some of the missing people below ground."

"There are missing people?" the cop asked, in a tone that sounded insincere. The few people she spoke to regularly from within the department were open about the City's official non-involvement, but perhaps it was quiet enough in the neighborhood to afford complete deniability.

"There are always missing people, Sergeant," she said.

"Why did you call the owners the day before?" he asked.

"My deal with the Thundertown organizer was to open an entrance between the City and the Underground. If we were to dig mechanically, the process could take weeks, so I assumed that he would use a design to build a tunnel overnight. With that in mind, I used common-sense safety precautions and evacuated one isolated spot, in case the worse should happen."

"So you were doing everything by the book."

She nodded.

"Would you mind if I got your statement?"

"No, I have to see if the exit is intact."

He nodded. "You do that. What else?"

"I need to measure the damage."

"I can have measurements for you. Do your thing, and meet me back at the command post. You know where it is."

She shed her legs again once he was gone and lowered her tail down the side of the hole, feeling the edges for a grip. Her tail inched around a length of pipe jutting out of the ground a few feet down and grabbed it. She tested its strength, judged it sturdy, and began to lower herself hand over hand down into the hole. The wall was cold, mud wet and stones hard under her hands. Her coat was instantly streaked with mud. Whenever another foot of muscle slid down behind, her weight changed, knocking her off-balance. Twice she slipped, twice she caught her balance and kept moving. When she was level with her grip and had most of her body balanced rope-like over the pipe, she turned away from the wall to scan the surface. Across from her, on the north wall, was a huge, sagging hole. She climbed hand over hand to the lip, ignoring the cold spray, then dragged herself inside with her tail stretched behind her like a lifeline. Finally she was far enough inside to let go of the pipe and reel herself in.

She took a minute to catch her breath, then peeked out of the tunnel to see if there were enough handholds to climb up. Finding none, she called her office to call the police department for Sergeant Jones' number, and through that complicated branching phone call, got an officer to unroll a rope ladder onto the tunnel's bottom lip. While she waited, she took in the gentle downward slope heading west into the island, sturdy and flat enough for feet to walk across. It was wide enough for four people, and if she remembered correctly, it coincided with a maintenance tunnel for the old Croton Reserve. If it didn't collapse after breaching the surface, it would have been a huge improvement over the uneven and slippery floor of the first tunnel.

Sergeant Jones took her statement in the command post as promised, then gave her the department's information on the disaster. In return, she sketched out an estimate of the size and depth of the tunnel.

When they were done, she summoned up the Kijkaan's image. As her eyes adjusted to the textured darkness, she was surprised to find him in his office.

"Kijkaan," she called out.

She was answered by a long, dragging snore.

"Kijkaan!"

The snoring cut off abruptly, and slowly the two beams of light appeared. "Miss Loisaida?"

"Good morning."

"Is it morning?" He stifled a yawn. "What— what's happening?"

"Tell me where I am."

One light went out as he rubbed his eye. "It looks like you're out by the river— are you at the exit site?"

"I am. Can you tell me why?"

He didn't answer.

"Because the tunnel you built here collapsed."

He sat in silence for half a second. "Don't you dare say this is my fault."

"No?"

He slapped the table. "This was your idea! I already had a safe way to get people out of Alvarville!"

"You still did this."

"We both knew this job was fraught."

Loisaida chose not to respond.

"Building in Manhattan isn't easy," he pushed.

When it was clear no apology was forthcoming, she cut him off. "You need to fix this."

"With what? How? There are so many companies with underground pipes and wires that I'd spend the next year on the phone looking for permission to build! You need to go to the City yourself and appeal for assistance."

"No. This is your responsibility."

"No! It's yours!" he roared. "It's your territory, your idea, your contacts— all yours!"

"I didn't make it fall."

"Good luck proving *I* did!" He cut the call short, causing a sharp sting between her eyes. She caught her balance on a wall and waited for the pain to subside before looking for Sergeant Jones and the site owner. She handed them the Kijkaan's card when she found them.

"Do I need to tell you not to say this name out loud?" she asked. They shook their heads. "Thank you. This is the contact information of the person who I believe is responsible for what happened."

"Do you have any proof?" Jones asked.

"No."

He shrugged, tucked his hands into his pocket, and looked away. The owner took the card out of her hand with skepticism.

"I'm going to find it," she snapped.

She called into the office to tell them she would have to take a few days off to investigate the Kijkaan's contacts below-ground, then called a cab.

Chapter Fourteen

"SENATOR LOISAIDA CLOSED the tunnel."

Nails was sitting at the kitchen table at the Gross House, which was worse then he'd ever seen; there were lumps of mold on the floor and the walls. They were like wads of lace made out of meat.

"What are you talking about?" he asked. Alex was sitting at the table with his hand in his chin, eyes closed and unresponsive.

"Senator Loisaida closed the tunnel," he repeated.

"What tunnel?" Nails asked. The Kijkaan was sitting at the table with them, although something was making it difficult to see his face.

"The tunnel out of here."

NAILS WOKE UP and sat upright. He was still underground. The streetlamps buried awkwardly into the stone floor were still on, and the market was still mostly empty, although it seemed to be filling up with new tables.

The small man with the military gear waved at him as he wheeled his cart into the market.

"You survived the night!"

Nails smiled sheepishly. "Guess I did. Hey, quick question, how do you get back to the City?"

"If I send you to one of my spots, they'll act dumb because they don't know you. I'm really sorry. You're not the first person I've talked to. There's a Lord that's trying to open legal entryways to the City, maybe that'll be ready soon."

Nails thanked him and went to find some food, shopping for useful items as he went. He had vague memories of what was important on camping trips with his father, and slightly sharper memories of different survival guides he'd read during his pro-apocalypse phase, but he wasn't sure how much of it applied down here. Was a half-built underground city more like a camping ground, a desert, or a forest? It didn't even follow the traditional rules of a cave, with all the lights, trashcans, and water fountains scattered around. He bought some food that wouldn't spoil, a lighter, and some matches. He knew he'd need water as well. By then, he was out of money, and he walked back to camp still not sure if anything he bought was going to help.

The group was getting ready to leave. Some of them were out buying the same snack food breakfast he'd picked up, while others were eating trail mix and beef jerky out of their bags, but everyone was folding their belongings and getting ready to move.

"Which direction are you going?" Rich asked.

"I'm coming with you. I don't want to go anywhere alone," he muttered.

Cassandra shot him a significant look over Rich's shoulder. A flash of anxiety warned him that none of them trusted him, that he'd done everything wrong to be part of the group, that they were going to watch him the rest of the way there. His anger followed and he thought, *Let them.* He wasn't here to make friends.

"The next settlement's in half a mile," Cassandra explained, as they began to walk.

He was still shaken, but the relief of a direct invitation soothed some of it. He fell in line with Rich and tried, hesitantly, to connect. "So, where'd you get that coat?"

"Down here. I wasn't wearing one when the train went off the rails. What do you think? Think it could use some studs?"

"Sure, it's like cowpunk."

Rich's head whipped around. "What is *cowpunk*?"

"It's like, um, country and punk," he said awkwardly, then quickly changed the topic. "Hey, can I ask you where we're going? Like, how does she know where to go?"

"We asked for directions. Navigating is a little weird down here. Most of these tunnels are new, and everyone who lives down here is still used to traveling above ground, so even though nothing lines up with the grid, people will still tell us to walk to 34th and 8th, or Lexington. And what's even weirder is that.... OK, so we're leaving 59th street, and we're going to pass the Minetta exit we were talking about last night. That's downtown, on the west side. Then, to get to the Kijkaan's place on 181st street, we're going to the east side past Avenue A and then skip the whole island to walk through the Bronx before we get there."

Nails sketched out the image in his mind. "So how long's it gonna take us?"

"A couple hours, maybe. It might take a day if we need to rest."

"Oh," Nails said.

A few minutes later, there was the sound of rushing water.

"That's the Minetta creek," Rich said.

The map in Nails's head turned upside down and scattered the landmarks he put there. He knew what the walk from 59th street to the West Village felt like, and it was never that fast. Maybe Rich was messing with him.

They passed another bend with a few small houses in it. One was big enough for a human, but the next one was a kid's playhouse installed on the rock. The rest was a doll-sized city carved right into the raw cavern wall. He could see small lights in windows, and as he watched, an enormous millipede wearing an appropriately-sized fedora came out of one hole, climbed into another, and turned a light off behind it.

The sound of rushing water built up then got softer and then vanished.

"Where's the creek?" he asked.

"Above us," Rich explained. "How do you know Sam?"

"We got a lot of friends in common and go to the same shows. She's good people."

"She is. Is she a lesbian?" Rich asked.

"Yeah."

"I thought so."

"She makes it pretty obvious," Nails muttered.

"I can't tell anymore. Kids these days dress like that for attention," Rich said. Nails rolled his eyes and turned up the elevator music in his head. Meanwhile, Rich was still going in full force. "I mean, look at hipsters. They dress like gay hobos, but they work at Google and make a couple hundred thousand annually."

"Are you saying everyone who works at Google dresses like a gay hobo?" Horace asked, swinging into the conversation.

"Present company excluded."

"Maybe I don't know what a gay hobo looks like."

"Scarf, beanie, hasn't shaved in three days—"

"*You* haven't shaved in three days."

"It's all part of my new look. I'm going for this style the kids are calling 'cowpunk'." He winked at Nails. "So what kind of punk are you?"

"I'm just trendy," Nails said.

"Can you be both?" Rich asked.

"Well, *I* am."

This lead to a conversation about the definition of a trend, and whether it was restricted to the mainstream or could take place in smaller populations. Meanwhile, they entered the market, which was set in a sunken stone amphitheater. The uneven steps spiraled down into a small, bare center, and tables were forced to balance their legs on spare parts.

"How many of these markets are there?" Nails wondered.

"There's really only six or seven markets," Rich said.

"This place isn't that big; we've seen it all three times in a month," Horace said.

"So, you got a cute punk rock girlfriend waiting at home?" Rich asked.

"Nah."

"More than one?" He laughed. "How many?"

"There's nothing going on," Nails said. It wasn't true, but it was easy to say. As much as he wanted them to like him and trust him, there was a complicated knot sitting in his stomach that he didn't want to untangle. It started with a single thread and built up every day, string by string until it was at his throat. It was always there, under the surface, constant enough to forget, but always present.

He wanted to talk about it, but he didn't want to talk about it. Saying it out loud was going to change him, the way people saw him and the way he saw himself, and even though he knew plenty of people who existed on the other side, it was hard for him to go there.

He wished he wasn't the person he was, who made the decisions he did. He liked people who looked good and struck up conversations with people he wanted to look at, and that steered him well for most of his life. Things usually worked out. He didn't think too deeply about it until he started hanging out with Alex a little too long and realized he really liked looking at him and wound up a situation where the person he was closest to was the person he needed to talk about to someone.

It should have been easy to fall for a person who was already out, already happy with themselves, but it wasn't. It should have been easy because they were already close, but instead, he felt like the person responsible for maintaining their relationship. One wrong move and it was over.

"You sure?" Rich asked.

"Yes, dude."

"There's nobody you're interested in?" Horace pressed.

"What, would you know them if I told you?"

"That means there is," Horace decided.

"Is it Sam?" Rich asked.

"Dude, no."

THE FLASHLIGHTS ALL started to sputter as soon as they were out of sight of the basement. Long shadows darkened and swallowed up the beams of light as Alex was trying to walk. He took small steps, trying to make as much use of their light as he could. Mika had never checked her flashlight's batteries before, and Bonnie's was missing a battery latch. The tape she used to hold the batteries in place was cracked. She had to hold them in place with her palm. Together they crowded around Magi to light his grimoire while he searched for the Design he used in the House. Most of his designs were copied from a public domain alchemy textbook written in the 18th century, which leaned its weight on the theory that the Aether was an inherently combustible substance. Based on the theory of phlogiston, the writer believed that every student should begin their studies by manipulating the mechanical process of ignition to produce a kind of fireball. This, he felt, would give them a physical sense of the fabric of the universe.

The orb of white light buoyed up as soon as it was summoned, then lazily drifted to the floor, rolling in circles around their feet. The surface of the orb was warm to the touch and left a lingering heat in their fingertips. Magi tossed it up in the air and watched it drift slowly down. Sam batted it back up, a light breeze re-directed it to Bonnie, who sent it spinning slowly downward. Alex caught it in the center of his palm and sent it flying up to the ceiling.

THE ROCKY GROUND beneath them dipped and rose erratically. The shiny, bubbly deposits of minerals ended sharply in a wide, flat chamber covered in a carpet of rust, as sharply divided as the tunnel and the Card House basement. Magi stopped to scuff the line with his toe. Beneath the rust were two equal shelves of rock.

"I wonder where we are," he muttered.

"We're underground," Bonnie pointed out.

"I mean besides that," Magi said. "Where in the City, where in Thundertown. And what was this cave built for? Is it natural? Do they grow this big, or was it built by Folk? Or Humans?"

"I want to know where we're going," Mika said.

"Sam, where are we going?" Bonnie shouted.

Sam ignored her.

"Sa-MAN-tha!" she shouted.

Sam flinched. "We should stay quiet."

Bonnie bared her teeth. "Does that mean we're walking blindly through some hole in the ground for days on end without plans? Is the whole idea to wait for something to jump us?"

"Maybe nothing finds us if we're quiet," Sam grumbled.

"We need a *plan*!" Bonnie shouted.

"I think we should stop and ask for directions," Mika said sarcastically.

"*You* can ask for directions," Bonnie snapped. "*I* think we should call Loisaida."

Sam sighed. "This road goes somewhere."

"Yeah, sure, it probably does, but for how long do we have to walk until we reach it? Who says it's safe, wherever we're going? How long are we going to keep going until we accept that we're lost and try again, later, with more information? That's the only smart thing we can do at this point."

The only sign that Sam was listening was a pulse in her jaw as she gritted her teeth.

They kept walking, the only sound coming from the snow-like crunch of the rust underfoot.

"If you were smart, you'd turn around before Loisaida closes that hole behind us."

Up ahead, a light bloomed. Sam met Bonnie's eyes.

Her expression remained neutral. "We can't tell what that is."

A little closer, they found the light attached to a shed, with a Plexiglass window, a mouthpiece, and a rotating Plexiglass box on the counter for exchanges. Inside, a small man in a button-up collar worked on a crossword at a cluttered desk. The fluorescent light made him look like a fish in a bowl, alone in an environment alien to his surroundings.

Sam knocked on the glass.

The man spared her a tired glance, then went back to his crossword puzzle. "Yes?"

"Could you help us?"

"That depends."

"What's this booth for?" Alex asked.

Without looking up, he pointed his pen to a spray-painted sign on the side of the shed that said PROPERTY OF GRENDELMEN SECURITY LLC. Underneath it was a crude shield with a crescent in one corner.

"What are you securing?" he asked.

"The site."

"What fucking site?" he grumbled, as Magi moved forward to interrupt.

"Did you have an attack golem on-site?"

He nodded. A second passed before he looked up from his crossword. "You tangle with it?"

"Yes, sir."

He ran his teeth over his lip. "Where is it?"

"It's in the office of the Lady Loisaida," Bonnie said. "You have to talk to her if you want it."

The man dragged a notepad over his crossword puzzle. "Spell that for me?"

She laid the business card on the bottom of the box and rotated it for him to copy.

While he was writing, Alex asked, "Who manages this site?"

"The Van Aarde firm."

That meant nothing to him. He could only guess through context that it was a Folk firm, although with the amount of information he had, he wouldn't have been shocked if they were human.

Sam stepped in next; "Where's the closest market?"

He flicked his pen over his shoulder. "Head west, to the 59th street market. That's the closest one that's definitely open."

"That's nowhere near here," Magi said.

"No, that's nowhere near where you *were*. Now you're in Brooklyn, under Court Street, and I'm telling you the 59th street market is the closest one to us."

"What the fuck," Sam muttered, but the man wasn't forthcoming with answers. He only shrugged.

"Thank you," Alex said, finally.

The little man met his eyes with a kind of worn-out disgust. "Don't."

THE NEW TUNNEL they found themselves in was wide, well-lit, and paved, but empty and unused.

Soon, they reached a police barricade, and after they all agreed their only instructions were to keep going west, stepped over it. The cave was half-finished on the other side of the barricade, unpolished, many of the lamps unlit, many not installed. Beyond that was raw cave, marked with arrows and notes left by the construction crew. Magi lit another fireball.

Past another barrier, there was nothing but layers of rock that bulged and sagged with heavy mineral sediment. The path grew narrower, forcing them to walk in single file. Soon they were shuffling sideways between two rough walls bristling with clusters of brown quartz that caught and reflected the orb of light on thousands of faucets and snagged on their coats.

Finally, they squeezed out one by one onto another broad, paved, lit road. Around them, foot traffic streamed toward a bright doorway, where they could see vendors and shoppers milling around a circular stone room with a low ceiling, full of the dull roar of conversation.

"Congratulations, Sam, you found us a market," Bonnie said. "After we get some supplies and rest up, what's our next step?"

Sam frowned. "We sit."

Alex pointed ahead to an arrangement of what looked like broken park benches. They weaved through and relaxed in silence, taking in the feeling of being off their feet. Sam shrugged off her backpack and rolled her shoulders, cracking vertebrae.

Bonnie jogged her foot. "When are we going to start?"

Sam shrugged and continued to stretch her shoulders.

"What do we do if nobody knows anything?"

"Move on. Keep asking."

Bonnie glared.

She shrugged. "Go home if you don't like it."

"It's too late for any of us to go home, so stop saying that," Mika said.

She shrugged again and went back to stretching.

"What about a spell? This is the place to get them, right? We can buy a homing beacon spell or something to find your friends with."

Magi's head popped up at the word 'spell,' but then quickly lowered again, as if remembering something embarrassing. "Oh, uh, actually, spell isn't the right term. A Design is a formula used to cause a response in the Aether, not a spell."

She looked at him with extreme distaste. "You knew what I meant."

"I'm trying to help. If people hear you asking for spells and magic, they can tell you're not familiar with them."

"I'm not stupid," Bonnie said with a growl.

He folded in a little more. "I'm only saying that because a lot of people get burned buying 'spells' because there's no regulation on them. That's not the official terminology anymore, so when people go looking for—"

"Let's go shopping. We all need food and water," Alex interrupted.

Sam threaded her arms back through the handles of her bag and stood, pausing to clap Magi on the shoulder.

"Don't worry 'bout her."

Alex got up to follow her, but when he glanced back, he saw Mika lean into his shoulder.

He shopped with one eye out, to keep a sense of where the others were. Bonnie went from booth to table tightly wound, shoulders near her ears and fists balled tightly. Sam was turning every conversation into an interrogation, staring down vendors who all looked for ways to escape. He caught sight of Magi and Mika book shopping, gingerly flipping through grubby old Aether design textbooks that turned their own pages and spit pennies as they were read.

There was an old-fashioned, wood hotdog stand selling regular bottles of water for two bucks, and a free-running fountain in the center of the market where people collected water. He weighed his options; the fountain was a pipe over a pit lined with concrete. He bought a bottle.

He passed a shopping cart parked against the wall, covered in bags and pouches in olive drab, desert beige, and camo in every style, from tiger stripe to pixel. Sitting on the side was a very small man sewing a patch onto a fringe jacket. The little man nodded, and Alex nodded back, still browsing the top of the cart. Pushing aside a rusty canteen, two rifle magazine pouches, and a handful of knives, he found a second layer of camping equipment.

A cloud of mothballs and salt rose up when he pushed the surplus gear out of the way. Wrinkling his nose, he grabbed a few dented boxes of fire starters and collapsible cooking instruments, then reached for two boxes of water filters. One of them turned to dust in his hand and he struggled to pick the filters out before they sank deeper into the cart. The little man dropped his sewing and immediately jumped to the lip of the cart.

"Relax, I've got it," he said. He pushed two children's books aside and plucked the last two filters out of the crevice they settled in. "I'll give you a deal on these."

"How much?"

The little man squinted thoughtfully. "Forty?"

"For... everything?"

"That's right."

It was a good price for the amount of stuff he'd get, but it would come close to cleaning him out. He solemnly put two collapsible pans back.

"What's the matter?" the man asked, holding it up. "Do you want these?"

He said nothing, wondering what else he could sell when his US currency ran out. Sam approached, looked first at the pan, then the vendor, then raised an eyebrow at Alex.

"I could give you the set for 30," the man offered.

Sam met Alex's eyes and shook her head. "We don't need them."

The final total came to twenty, and as he scraped out the money, he caught sight of the patch the man was sewing onto the collar of his jacket—an embroidered patch, similar to the military patches on other parts of his jacket, but with a skull and a sword instead.

"Do you listen to that band?" he asked.

The little man searched the area around his seat for whatever prompted Alex to ask that question. "What band?"

"From that patch," he said.

The little man looked down at his jacket. "This is a band?"

Alex paused. Knife Wound started out as a parody band but was rapidly gaining genuine popularity. They were created to be the prototypical New York Punk Band, an intentional grab-bag of repeating patterns that kept popping up in new music. People outside of New York either loved them or hated them for being self-aware, but they made no sense to people who weren't familiar with their source material.

Nails was at their show two weeks earlier.

"Where did you get that?" he asked.

"I let some kid trade me a bag for it."

Alex's heart thumped. "Who?"

He shrugged. "Some kid. Tall, white and skinny."

"Did he look tired? Did he have really bad fingernails, like covered in open scabs?"

The man looked genuinely surprised. "Yes, actually. It was kind of gross."

Alex looked up at Sam. Her expression was stone.

The man at the booth threw his jacket into his cart and began to rise. "Look, I don't want any trouble—"

"We won't give you any," Alex promised.

"No, I mean— I don't know anything. There's nothing I can tell you."

"You see where he was going?" Sam asked.

"No. And I didn't ask."

"Didn't see which direction they went?"

"Them and a few others camped out on those benches over there for a night— maybe you could catch up with them."

"Wait, what about a homing beacon spell— design— thing?"

"I don't do that." The man warned, kicking the lock mechanism off his cart.

Alex scrambled for the right words to keep him with them. "Who does?"

"You should check the Minetta street market. Your friend went that way, anyway."

Sam held out her hand. "I want one more thing; I was also looking for a weapon."

He looked at her with guarded interest. "You gonna pay?"

"Yeah."

He hesitated briefly, but any reluctance was tempered by her promise. He kicked the lock down and parked the cart. "What do you want? A gun? Samurai swords?"

"You got those?" Alex asked.

"Guns, yes, but no ammo."

Sam shook her head. "No, no, I want something that'll work."

"That's a pretty broad spectrum of things. How much are you looking to pay?"

"I could give you a tattoo," she offered.

"No, thanks."

She shucked off her jacket, rolled up the cuffs of her sleeves, then bent down and rolled up her pants. "I got ink on both arms and legs. I'm not giving up the half-finished piece on my back. Good enough?"

His eyes skimmed her arms, touching his lip in thought. He turned her arm, bent down, and poked at a crow on her ankle, then faced the cart, still tapping his lip. "Not a tattoo on me, huh?"

She shook her head. The little man stood there, with his hand on his cheek, then dug his fingers into the cart's grates and climbed inside. He pushed back the layer of army surplus and camping gear, grabbed something with both hands, and gave it a strong pull. He cursed and wheezed as he pulled, struggling to drag it up from the depths. Sam grabbed the top and pulled with him, while Alex did his best to loosen the knot of wires and straps around it. As they pulled, they unearthed one long, sturdy bone, as smooth and strong as marble. Straight lines were cut and sanded into the thinner ends as a grip, with a small, straight nick at the thick end. It was the length of an entire arm, with a socket on one end and a long, flat head on the other. The man handed the bone to Alex, then slowly began pulling out a second one, exactly like the first. Panting and sweating, he yanked it free and held it up. On the flat, knotted head was a plus sign.

"I tell you what," he said, leaning on his cart to catch his breath. "For the crow on your leg, I'll trade you these;

you're one of the few people down here who would appreciate them."

"What are they?" Alex asked. When he touched it, his skin tingled with electricity.

"Horse femurs."

Sam took the second bone from him and turned it over in her hands, reverent. "What do they do?"

The man tapped his fingernail against the head of the bone with the cross. An arch of white-hot lightning jumped high up and connected with his finger. Then, more gingerly, he flicked the dash. There was a rumbling bang, and his arm jerked back. Vibrations shook Sam's arm. Her eyes widened.

The man massaged his elbow. "Thunder and lightning."

"Where did you get these?" Alex asked.

"I made them," he answered proudly. "I did some work for a guy upstate; he did all the sanding and carving. We made a great rig for his farm. Bone's a great conductor for Aether."

"They're beautiful," Sam breathed.

He beamed. "It really is. You should see the setup he has, but I don't really need these, because... Well, it does what I already do. And a lot of the Folk around here feel the same way I do— they're nice, but nobody needs them."

Sam grinned. "But I do."

He smiled back. "But you do! What do you think, sound fair?"

Sam ran her hands up and down the side of the bone.

"It was my first tattoo," she said, then quickly added, "My first good tattoo."

She set the bone down. "How are we doing this?"

"Lift up the leg again," he said. She leaned against the wall for balance and let him pick up her calf. He looked past the tattoo, at the meat, poking and stretching the skin thoughtfully.

"Hmm... Shouldn't be too hard. It's right on the calf, not too close to the bone or any arteries... Give me a minute." He pulled a pen out of his cart and drew a messy circle all around the piece, pulled the skin taut to check his work. "It's gonna hurt, but you're tough, right?"

"What're you going to do?" Alex asked.

"Well, I'm going to force the skin off," he said, poking at the flesh around the tattoo. "Basically, I'm going to grow new skin under this circle, and try to push the tattoo off in one solid sheet. Normally, the skin would flake off over the course of years, so I want a couple decades' worth of skin to grow straight up from the tissue. It'll be clean- you could probably even get another tattoo in the same place—but it's going to hurt like a bitch."

She nodded. "Let's do it."

Alex grabbed her shoulder. She gave his hand a squeeze in response.

The man spread a blue tarp on the floor in front of his cart, then rolled a foam yoga mat down for Sam to sit on. They both positioned her leg so that she could rest comfortably while giving him access to the raven. She waited for him to finish twisting her ankle left to right, lining up the tattoo with the light in the cave. As she closed her eyes to prepare, he stepped away.

"Wait." He went back to his cart and sifted through his things, finally producing a brass bullet with a flat, dull head on a chain. "Take this."

She dangled it from her hand. It looked like a normal bullet, empty, with a hole carved through the bottom of the shell for the chain. "What's this for?"

"Biting," he said. She stuck the bullet between her teeth. Alex's fingers curled into his bag.

He adjusted her leg a little more, then fished a handful of pins out of the cart and slid them under her skin, around the edge of the circle. She hissed and bit down.

"That's the easy part," he warned. His fingers glowed until the bones stood out in silhouette. Goosebumps broke out all over Sam's skin. Hair rose on Alex's head. The man traced the pins with his fingers, and the little circle of metal turned white hot, searing through her flesh. Her face turned red and glistened with beads of sweat. Her teeth ground down on the bullet, fists squeezing until the knuckles turned white. She closed her eyes and howled around the bullet in her teeth. The smell of burning rose up from the mat.

Finally, the man took his hands off her. "OK— you're done."

Her elbows buckled, and she collapsed. She panted while the man removed pins whistling with heat from a steaming slab of pink meat. The skin left behind on her calf was as smooth and shiny as it would be in the shower.

"See? Easy," the man said cheerfully, and tossed her skin, crow and all, into his cart. Sam tried to push herself upright, but the heels of her hands scraped uselessly against the ground. Alex dropped his bag to catch her and push her into a sitting position. Shaking and bleary, she fished a bandanna out of her back pocket and used it to wipe the sweat out of her eyes. She tried to clean the taste of copper out of her teeth, spat twice, then slowly rose to her knees, bracing herself against the wall. Alex ducked his head under her arm and helped her gently to her feet.

"You look great," the man promised, holding out the two smooth brown bones. She almost lost her fragile balance when she reached for them, but the man and Alex coordinated a way to keep her upright.

He added two cheap canvas holsters to the sale and helped string them around her hips to hold the bones.

She looked down at the chewed-up bullet around her neck and her new army surplus holsters full of bones. "Damn."

The man gave Alex a stern look. "Make sure she doesn't go wandering off and get some food in her."

Alex fit Sam's bag over her shoulder and her arm around his neck and slowly walked her back to the park benches. Her head dropped as they walked, and her weight fell across Alex's back as she began to fall asleep.

"Sam!" he cried, buckling under her. "Sam, c'mon, you have to stay awake."

She tried to take her arm back and curl away from him, forcing him to pull against her. "I'm getting you food. Wait till we sit down so you can watch the bags, OK?"

She gave him a thumbs up. Finally he let her collapse on the stone park benches, where she curled onto her side and fell asleep instantly. He bolted back into the market, scanning every table for food. Finally, he found one stall selling bread, bought a loaf, and hustled it back to the park benches.

She responded when he shook her, but drowsily, and nodded off again when he sat down to break off some dry, crumbling chunks of bread. He forced her to eat. Her eyelids beat rapidly as she struggled to stay awake. After a long drink of water, the white very gradually left her face.

"We need to go," she said, at last.

"We need everybody else," he pointed out.

She forced herself to finish the last hunk of bread. "Where are they?"

From the circle of benches, they could see Bonnie arguing with someone at a stall, and on the other side of the market, the back of a blonde head which might have been Mika, but without Magi.

Sam unhooked one bone from her holsters and held it up, shining the light on the smooth grain. She gave it an experimental swing, which changed the air pressure around them like a storm.

When the others came back, they took inventory. The first words out of Bonnie's mouth were directed to Sam. "Where are we going?"

"We're going to the Minetta Street market for a locator design," Sam said, grabbing her bag.

Chapter Fifteen

IN HALF A mile, they were under Minetta Street, standing above the stepped bowl of the market. Sam and Alex walked down, while the others stayed on the edge.

Alex was walking straight to the bottom to look up at the market, but before he got there, a thin, reedy voice shouted from nearby.

"Ah! Ah! You! Ragazzo! Boy! Viene qui!"

A small figure under an enormous shawl was waving for his attention, sitting on an old Persian rug laid out over the stairs. The face inside the shawl was a little off— shiny and flat, like a Halloween mask. She beckoned him closer, lower, until he was crouched down in front of her, eye to eye. She reached down and grabbed his hand, twisting it around to spread his palm. He noticed immediately that the knuckles were all wrong, and she didn't seem to have any fingernails.

"I see something about you that I have not seen before," she said, tracing her hand over his palm. "Something in your past that is special..."

He rolled his eyes and tried to politely take his hand back. "Thanks, I'm not interested."

She pulled him back with a strength he didn't expect. "Your family, where are they from?"

"Don't you know that?" he asked, trying again to slip away. She grabbed his wrist and pulled him down. "Let me go!"

"You have a strong family line, here," she said. "Great things have happened."

"I'm Puerto Rican, lady."

"A long and hard history," she said. "You should be proud."

"I didn't say I wasn't, I told you to let me go!"

"*Hey!*" Sam barked. The old woman suddenly released him, buried her hands in the shawl, and began to weave weakly in the folds. "What's your problem?"

"Scusame, me dispace," she said, straining her voice to be even thinner and weaker. "I am in tune to the Aether, I do not always behave as I should."

"Bullshit. Alex, you all right?"

"I'm all right." He muttered, getting off the floor.

"Wait," the old woman said. "Wait—please, I want to make friends. I want to do a favor for you."

"No, thanks," Sam said, grabbing Alex's shoulders and steering him away. "Somebody recognized Leticia. Said they passed through, but didn't stop."

"Let's find somebody who can do a locator and then get the fuck out of here."

Sam took a few steps up to reach the eye level of a stall above them and asked who was doing design work.

"The only person doing that is Donna Pirdunu." He said and pointed straight across the bowl at the shawled figure.

"Anybody else?" Alex asked.

He shrugged. "Most people here can do it themselves."

"Fuck," Alex said. They walked down the stairs and stopped in the small square at the bottom of the stairs.

"We could go somewhere else," Sam said.

"Where?" he asked. They walked back up the stairs to Donna Pirdunu. The eyes in her strange, smooth face were wide and hungry.

"Ah, this is interesting," she said, then closed her eyes and put one hand to her head. "There's something— something about you— no, no, it's the boy—"

"I get it," Alex said. "We heard you do design work."

She didn't answer immediately. The interruption seemed to have thrown her off, and she sat blinking in confusion.

"I sense," she tried again. "A great power—"

"We heard," Alex said. "You told us that. We were here five minutes ago."

She frowned. "Impossible, I am here all day."

Alex opened his mouth to argue, then changed his mind. "Listen, Donna Pirdunu, we need a design. Can you help us?"

A smile lit her face. "You've heard of me?"

"Oh yeah," he said. "And we need you to make a locator design for us."

She kept smiling. Inside the plastic mask of her face, her small yellow eyes seemed to burn. "Of course. Give me the name."

She fished inside her shawl for a warm felt pen and a small, warped notebook. Alex wrote Nails's full name onto the paper. She took the page and the pen from him and began to write. The rhythm of her pen scratching on the paper began slow, then picked up speed until she was making broad, sharp scratches on sheet after sheet of paper. She stopped and flipped rapidly back to the first page, then tore every single written page out of the notebook. She laid them out in a grid, fished a roll of tape out of her shawls, and taped them all into place. Then she opened the notebook again and began writing down an equation, a small, wet red tongue peeking through her lips when she concentrated. Then she crushed them in the center, balled it all up and stuffed it into a cheap drawstring bag.

"For you," she said, but when he reached out to take it, she snatched it back with a watery, mischievous smile. "Now, payment."

"Twenty bucks?" he offered.

She shook her head and a finger in opposite rhythms. "No, no, no. I think you have something more valuable for this. Is your friend worth twenty bucks?"

"What do you want?" he demanded.

"I smell something special. Where is it?"

"I don't know what you're talking about."

The old woman hummed tunelessly and touched her hand to her head. "I see a little girl in a white dress. Beautiful. Strong."

"That's my aunt," Alex snapped

She dangled the pouch. "For your friend?"

He snatched it out of her hand and threw a twenty into her lap.

She sat up on her knees. "Thief! Thief! I'm robbed! Ay, aiutome, i mostri, loro uccidime!"

They reached the top of the market and ran over to the group.

"What did you do?" Bonnie demanded.

"Don't worry about it, it's fine, let's go," he said and tossed the pouch to Magi. "Tell us where to go."

Magi turned the pouch over curiously, then opened it and looked inside. "What is this? Why is it ripped up?"

"I don't know, you're the expert. It's supposed to be a locator spell."

"You mean a design," he corrected, then shrugged. "Well, there's only one way to find out what it actually is."

He snapped his fingers. They all flinched.

Nothing happened.

Alex glanced back at the lip of the market. "Can we go?"

Magi opened one eye and inspected the pouch. "I think it worked. Let's start walking and hope for the best."

LOISAIDA PACKED A bag and took a cab downtown to the hole in the island. The first thing she did was scratch a design into the gravel around it to build a bridge from the exit to the street. Then, without waiting for it to form, she carefully lowered herself hand over hand down the hole. The surface of the cliff seemed to simmer as dirt rolled out of the riverbed and embedded into the wall. In a few hours, a crust should have formed that sturdy enough to carry at least one person. By the afternoon, it should be big enough for four or five to climb up to the City shoulder to shoulder.

When she reached the mouth of the cave, she let go of the wall and let the length of her tail collapse in a coil on top of her. The cavern was vaguely familiar— she couldn't remember clearly if she'd been in this passage before, or one very similar to it. It seemed to be an abandoned MTA break room, once buried and now excavated. There was a doorway that led to a square room that used to be tiled, with the dusty remains of furniture. One wall was scooped out to make way for a path deeper into the island. She recognized a few relics the farther she walked, catching sight of a basement she was definitely familiar with, and the remains of a sewer that used to service the old Croton

Reservoir. Soon she was at a familiar settlement, built out of shale, which gave it a chewed-up, papery look, like a wasps' nest. Someone had installed streetlamps between the houses in imitation of a street. As she walked in, she saw a familiar building. It was a carbon copy of a building that used to be in her neighborhood; there was the turn of the century brickwork, the die-cast floral accents, and through the door, she could see a checkerboard floor that she used to think of as iconic. A man was reading at the front desk, cheek propped up on his elbow. Behind him was a bar full of blue light, where two men played dominoes, while the bartender twisted a radio dial for a signal.

She almost stopped to talk to them, to ask them if they were happier here than in the City, but instead, she moved on.

The roads the Kijkaan built were sloppy and confusing. She recognized the outcroppings of civilization, but the roads were a mess. Bits and pieces from all over the City were forced together and tortured into an imitation of order. She walked from her neighborhood to Brooklyn, and suddenly found herself in the Minetta Street market. She asked there how la Donna Pirdunu was doing, and whether anyone was watching her or feeding her, but there was no news of anyone coming by to check on her. All she learned was Donna Pirdunu came to market and tried to sell designs. Sometimes she slept in the market.

It turned Loisaida's stomach to hear how much she'd decayed. Donna Pirdunu could be a good friend when she wanted to be. She was a little vain, a little superficial, but she liked to be that way. As the years went on and she got older, it was harder for her to keep score of who was in her good books. The last time Loisaida saw her, she didn't recognize Loisaida, and as they were arguing, she seemed to forget what they were talking about. Pirdunu began instead to confide in her that things were getting hard to recognize. Friends, family, enemies were all getting blurry. She was afraid.

Loisaida left Minetta Street and continued uptown, through the ridiculous and convoluted path the Kijkaan had built. Somewhere in the Bronx, she passed by a small, familiar figure.

"Donna Pirdunu?"

The old woman crumpled to the ground. Loisaida was familiar with this gambit and took a step back as Pirdunu threw off her shawl. She stretched to her full height, unfolding a body many times larger than her shawl. Her face was reminiscent of a human in its soft, sagging skin, but the bone structure was more pointed, pushed forward into a long nose and sharp golden eyes, glittering under a protective brow ridge. She still looked old and delicate, but now the bones of her fingers only made her claws look longer.

Loisaida held up her hands, palms out. "Mi Donna Pirdunu, bella e terrore. It's me, your student, Honora."

Pirdunu froze and teetered, off-balance. "Honora?"

"That's right. Baz's heir."

Pirdunu tilted her head to the side. "Baz's heir?"

Loisaida waited. As the minutes passed, it became clear that something was connecting, but not enough.

"Are you all right?" Loisaida pressed. "Are you far from home? Can I get you home?"

Pirdunu looked around her. Her expression spoke for her.

"Where are you staying?" Loisaida pressed.

"Thief," Pirdunu said at last. "I've been robbed. Thief! The bastards at the market watched and did nothing! They'll all pay."

"OK," she said. "Well, where are they now?"

"I slipped a tracker of my own into their design," Pirdunu said. "A simple thing. Now all it takes is to follow the path right to them."

"May I walk with you?" Loisaida asked. Hopefully they would catch up with Pirdunu's thief before their paths diverged, and Loisaida could help settle the problem without losing time to meet the Kijkaan.

Pirdunu faltered again, struggling to adapt to the new input.

"I'll come with you," she said, gently taking the old woman by the elbow.

ALEX NEVER SAW so many different types of rock before. They walked through an abandoned subway station covered in tilework. They passed a garden that was growing as if the sun was shining, a trailer park, empty hallways of smoothed limestone, high-traffic caverns of raw shale, and a suburb.

"How much further?" he asked.

"Not sure," Magi said.

The further uptown they got, the better the road was laid. Soon, they were walking on a wide path as flat as a sidewalk, and the ceiling was starting to rise. Ahead of them, they heard voices. Alex turned the corner expecting to see a new market, but instead, they entered a huge, empty cavern, where a group of people were standing, all staring at the ceiling.

"We're here," Magi said.

"Nails?" Alex asked. Nails stuck his head out of the crowd and grinned. He dropped his bag and started running. "No. Don't. Stop. David—"

Nails jumped on him, almost knocking him off balance. "You did it! You guys are not gonna believe this, but it's done, we're out of this shit! Sam— Sam— Sam, check it out, check it out—"

Nails grabbed Sam by the shoulders and steered her into the group. As they recognized her, they all began to shout and gather around her until she disappeared into it. Nails disentangled himself and danced back over.

"Do you recognize this place?" he asked Alex. "I bet you don't, but let me give you a hint."

He walked away from them and kicked something hard, small, and hollow on the floor. Alex, Magi, Mika, and Bonnie gathered around to look at the shattered plastic carcass of a cheap flashlight, the same one Alex dropped from the stairs leading to the Kijkaan's office. Alex looked up. There was nothing but condensation and darkness above them.

"So all we gotta do is get up there," Nails said.

Alex stared at him. When his smile didn't waver, he tried to prompt him to analyze the situation a little deeper. "That's it?"

"That's it!" he repeated. Alex gestures for more, and he shrugged. "We'll figure out a way up there."

"Like *what*?"

Nails shrugged again, a little defensive. "We gotta."

Sam's group absorbed them and the introductions began. There were so many names thrown at him that Alex didn't take in a single one. They were all a mass of happy smiling faces.

When he turned around, he found Loisaida standing in the cavern behind them, carrying a duffle bag over her shoulder.

"What are you doing here?"

"What are *you* doing here?" Loisaida countered.

"We were looking for Nails."

"I told you I could take care of that," she snapped. "What happened since you've been down here? What is going on, and what have you been doing?"

"Nothing?" he said. "We've been down here for like a day, maybe?"

"That's not what I heard," she said. "I'm coming from the Minetta Street market."

He responded to her tone with an annoyed and careless gesture. "And?"

"I think you know."

"I don't think I do."

"Tell me what happened," Loisaida demanded.

"What do you—"

Something punched through the mouth of the tunnel and sank into the wall, four sets of claws crushing the rock into pebbles. It had a face like an old woman and the matted hide of an enormous cat and turned its head as if to count them one by one.

Loisaida immediately pushed her way to the front of the crowd. "Donna mia, I need you to stop—"

Donna Pirdunu dropped to the ground and lunged at Loisaida, knocking her to the other side of the cavern.

"Shit—" Sam dropped her bag and unlatched a bone from her holster.

"Wait, you have no idea how those work," Alex warned.

"I can guess," she said and slammed the club straight down. A wooden sound reverberated off the cavern walls, and a crack of searing light cut through the darkness. Each rock in the tunnel stood out in stark relief of greys and black, except for one burning red splinter lodged into the back of the four-legged figure standing over Loisaida. A scream filled the cavern, and then the light went out.

"Advocabit," Alex said. He was aware that something was flying towards him; he could see a bright light and feel heat growing on his face. A fireball burned through the air towards him, but a little black girl in a white dress held the fire back with her bare hands, as sturdy in mid-air as she would be on land. He felt relief, and then a blow to his chest. He was slammed to the ground, the vinegar smell of animal fur filling his nose. He was face to face with a long, dark gullet, ringed in teeth. They stood out white and sharp with pockets of dark brown decay in their craters.

In his childhood memories, right after learning that Peter Stuyvesant burned trash and built the wall that Wall Street was named for, he learned the City was nearly strangled in its cradle by great Beasts. He used to be deeply, hypnotically fascinated by them; he lay awake at night trying to imagine being coaxed out of bed by a White Eyes, torn apart by a Rawhead, or drowned by the enormous Snake that lived in the island's only clean source of water. In the Natural History Museum was a small section on Great Beasts of the North Atlantic region, right after the beaver pelts and native birds display. The shapes of their skulls were surreal, their skins a constant threat. Although he knew the backgrounds were painted a hundred years ago, he was paralyzed with the idea that the glass would vanish and the Beast would come back to life.

Even dead, stuffed and mounted, being near them filled him with a primal fear.

He had forgotten that feeling.

There was a sharp click as Bonnie removed her safety, followed by the deafening hammer of shot after shot being fired into Donna Pirdunu's side. Some hit, others grazed, most landed in the rock around her, but each good blow thrashed her like a rag doll.

Pirdunu went stiff and collapsed to the floor.

The silence that followed was as painful as the shots that came before. Bonnie took a step closer.

Loisaida shouted and waved her arms, but the aftermath of the shooting rendered her silent.

Pirdunu's round, bleeding side rose as she filled her lungs. Her legs twitched, scratched the dirt, then pushed her onto shaking ankles. She narrowed her focus on Loisaida, her face twisted in a furious grimace.

"Beast!" Pirdunu roared.

A cold wind roared through the tunnel, lifted Donna Pirdunu, and threw her into a wall. Loisaida appeared and repelled Pirdunu with the same cold force. Alex, standing behind Lucinda, felt nothing but wind through his hair. Pirdunu was lifted off the floor and slammed into the wall behind them.

"Kijkaan!" Nails shouted up at the condensation above them.

Sam swung down with the bone in her hand as Pirdunu sprang up. The blow went wide, striking her in the shoulder instead of the face, but the lightning seared through her body, filling the cavern with the smell of burning hair and meat.

She collapsed before them with a deep, red gouge cut through her body, raking the dirt for balance.

Loisaida reached into the air and pulled. The atmosphere in the cavern changed, like an elevator going up. Inconsistent drumming filled the cavern. Rock broke from the walls all around them and whipped through the air, pounding the walls and floor. A stone struck Sam's side. Another caught Alex in the back of the head and pushed him face-first into a wall, forcing his teeth and nose back.

Stunned, bleeding, blind, he struggled to stand, but he was too dizzy to tell if he was on the floor, or still falling. He rocked like a sailor in a storm as he felt his face. There were a few cuts. His nose and two teeth were broken. His vision, when he opened his eyes, was fuzzy. He crawled away, desperate to escape, while the sounds of screaming filled the air.

Something sharp pinched him from under his armpits, and he lashed out blindly.

"It's fine, it's me," Magi whispered as he helped Alex to his feet.

His head swam behind his closed eyes. He rubbed his eyes hard enough to make tears fall, but still, his vision didn't stay clear. "What's happening?"

"I'm taking people out of the way," Magi explained, turning Alex around and pressing his back against a cold wall. "Wait here, I'll be right back."

"No—" Alex reached for his coat but only caught the rush of air behind him.

His mother taught him that the nasal bridge was soft, easy to break, and equally easy to shape. In theory, he could reset his own nose, but when he touched it, a new plateau of pain sprang up. He put his hands back on the wall, took a deep breath, and forced himself to open his eyes.

He was in the cavern entrance. From outside, he could see that the stones moved together like a flock of birds, diving in loops around the cavern. Nails was staring out from the safety of the other entrance. Sam was on the ground, protecting her head. Magi was trying to come back to Alex with the little girl in the pink jacket, and Bonnie was standing still and erect, taking blows to her head and abdomen while she lined up another shot.

All other noise stopped when the gun was fired. Concussive banging seemed to shatter the very air.

Alex's head rattled, first with the aftershocks of the explosion, and then with the pounding of rocks that all completed their final loop with a heavy crash. Donna Pirdunu was back on her side, screaming unheard.

As his hearing came back to him, Alex thought he could hear her, but then realized the sound, like nails on a chalkboard, was not coming from Donna Pirdunu. Loisaida was pulling a rusted flight of stairs out of the thin cloud cover of the cavern roof. Her mouth was open. He could make out the sound of her commanding them to get up and come over.

MAGI PICKED UP the little girl and ran towards the stairs. Nails was running towards Sam as she struggled to stand. Bonnie was oddly still. He left the safety of the cavern and ran to her— one hand was at her head and another at her stomach as if trying to hold herself together. She tightened up when he touched her. Horace appeared at his side and gestured as his lips moved, the muted sound of his voice giving context to his signals. He reached under her armpits, while Alex went to grab her knees.

Bonnie was buckling where she stood. She tried to tell them what was wrong, but neither of them could hear her. He could tell she was screaming. He felt the air change, like standing up after sitting down for too long, and a tornado of dust blew into the cavern, twisted like a string, tighten, then settle. A skeleton formed from the cloud, then two, and then skin grew and lashed them together. The construct from the Card House got down on its four legs and lunged at Donna Pirdunu as she tried to get up.

"*Now!*" Loisaida ordered.

He saw Donna Pirdunu closed her teeth down on one neck and crush the construct's collar bone. The construct dug its many fingers into Pirdunu's eyes. She spat its dry bones on the floor, pinned one arm with her hand and grabbed the other in her teeth.

The stairs touched down in front of Alex and Horace. The others were above them, making the slow climb to the office. Alex jumped onto the stairs and dragged Bonnie up behind him, while Horace collapsed behind him and clawed his way up

The stairs screamed as they rose. Donna Pirdunu looked up, with the construct's three remaining hands in her neck. She struggled to get up, but the construct held her back even while all its limbs snapped. Their battle became distant and faint, then disappeared beneath the condensation

"Are you OK?" Horace asked Bonnie.

Her hands and teeth were clenched in pain and fury, her face wet with tears and sweat. "*No!*"

They rested her on two of the stairs as carefully as they could. Alex let her squeeze his hand, but there reached a point when whatever comfort that offered was not enough, and she let him go again.

Once they'd reached the top, they lay Bonnie down. Loisaida cleared up Sam's concussion, mended her fractured shoulder, and reset a ligament in Magi's neck. Her attention shifted next to Bonnie.

Loisaida pushed her coat back, pulled up her shirt and bra to expose the dark bruise on her ribs. She pressed her fingers into the cage until she found the bone that swam away while Bonnie screamed. Loisaida steadied her breathing and pushed down, and sparks flashed in the air around them. Bonnie's screams broke into ragged gasps. Her legs kicked, then slowed, then settled into groggy stillness.

Loisaida pulled her bra and shirt back down and carefully watched for her reaction. Bonnie rubbed her forehead and moved as if to stand, then seemed to change her mind, and splayed out on the cold stone floor.

Loisaida rested her forehead on her knuckles to catch her breath, then turned to Alex. "Your turn."

"For what?" he asked. She grabbed his face, and with a sharp, bloody crack, his broken cartilage snapped back into place, and new teeth popped into old tooth beds like snapping a razor head off a box cutter. New pain blinded him again, washing his throat in fresh blood and clotted flesh. He choked off a scream and dug his nails into the palms of his hands.

She turned to Nails. "Next."

"Actually, I'm good," he said. She checked him anyway, and when she was satisfied, she turned to the door of the Kijkaan's door.

"Kijkaan," she called.

There was no answer.

"Kijkaan," she called again.

It became obvious that his office was open only by appointment.

"Now, Kijkaan. We're having our audience."

The only response was a ragged scream from Pirdunu, echoing from below. Loisaida tried to call him with his business card, but he, predictably, did not answer. At last, she unhitched the strap of the duffle bag, reached in, and removed what looked like a dry pink sponge.

"I have your employee!" she shouted.

There was no immediate response, but then there was the sound of a door unlocking. They were immediately assaulted by the smell of mold. In the dim light, soft, thin, hairlike filaments hung from the walls and ceiling in pale ringlets. Handfuls of young shoots stuck like corkscrews out of the wall, and the gills of adult mushrooms bristled in the corners. With the glamour peeled away, Alex could see there was no puce wallpaper with silver flecks and no tiles on the floor. It was still a hallway, with rooms leading off it, but now he could see that the doors rotted off years earlier, and what he first saw as an office was original, clearly, a storeroom. Sam led the way to the waiting room, where the furniture remained the way he remembered them, but still sunk in the carpet of mold.

"Disgusting," Cassandra said. At the end of a hallway, a door swung open.

"That's a little strong," the Kijkaan said on the other side, visible by the two pinhole lights shining deep in the office. "Do I need to remind you all that I just saved your life?"

"For a price," Loisaida said. She took the fleshy pink sponge out of the duffle bag and wet it with a dab of blood. With her other hand, she dug her fingers into the web of Aether wrapped tight around the shifter and tore it off.

With a ragged gasp, the dry flesh rose like bread. The shifter uncurled like a baby, arms and legs twitching stiffly as they stretched for the first time in days. With a sobbing, gasping breath, she turned herself over, and Loisaida quickly put her on a side table stacked with rotten magazines. Once the shifter caught her breath, she pushed herself up on four short protrusions and used them to drag herself forward. She reached the edge of the side table and fell, landing with a soft thud on the floor.

The Kijkaan held Loisaida's gaze the entire time.

"I hope now you'll give me an answer for the holes in my territory," she said. "According to your own red herring, no territory will be infringed on by any member of the Lord Beneath."

He smiled. "Should we fight in front of the kids?"

"There's no better time," she answered. "I was hoping to bring you the construct that was in the first tunnel you opened up, but I had to leave it downstairs."

"That reminds me—why did you bring a Beast to my doorstep?"

"Don't treat her like that. She's a confused old woman. I can handle her."

"That's not the impression I took away."

Bonnie took out the card from the construction site. "This is where that spider-man construct came from. They said the whole plot belonged to the Van Aarde firm."

"Who's Van Aarde?" Loisaida asked.

"Why are you doing this? What have I ever done?" the Kijkaan asked.

"Never mind," she said, putting the card in her purse. "I can find out later."

He made a noise between laughter and a scoff. "I'm sorry, are you or aren't you hiding in my office, under circumstances against my best interests? You can all go back to face that Beast for all I care."

Loisaida cocked her head. "Are you—"

But she didn't get the time to finish her sentence. She swallowed around something in her throat. Her hand rose up, and she coughed, small at first, but then louder and desperate. The air began to grow thick with the smell of mold and static, sucking the air right out of their lungs.

Mushroom gills flew open, and as Alex choked, he could taste mold growing like fur on his tongue. His eyes prickled as his chest grew tighter. His vision darkened. The Kijkaan seemed to retreat, sliding away from him as if on a dolly.

Two small lights appeared near him as he sunk down, his eyes full of swimming dust. As Lucinda stood over him, watching him sink, he felt sorry for himself, sorry for his mother, who sacrificed her own house block for nothing. Now Lucinda belonged to the Kijkaan, one of so many heirlooms passed into undeserved hands.

Through the cloying dizziness, he watched her reach out and slice through the frills of mold with the claw of her hand. He fell to the ground and cold, clean air filled his lungs. He raised his hand to point to where the others should be, hand shaking.

"Them, too."

She went next to Sam, then Nails, ripping through fungus-like spider-webs. The Kijkaan twitched, raised his hand and shot a blinding arch of fire at her. She didn't stop her task; instead, a second Lucinda appeared and caught it in the palm of her hand. Alex pushed himself upright on shaking hands and turned to face the Kijkaan. His chest burned, and every breath sounded like water in his lungs.

"Get out," the Kijkaan ordered. A tuneless note struck in the air, like a bow being fired, but whatever design he activated was caught and held hostage by Lucinda and her single, upturned hand.

"Get *out!*" he ordered. The air stirred as the Kijkaan worked up another design, but before he could fire it, Loisaida wound forward, whipped back her fist, and punched him in the temple. His head snapped back on his neck and he toppled behind the desk.

She glided around him, opened the cabinets, and leafed through them. As she read the pages in his cabinet, her resolve changed, and rather than sorting through them, she grabbed handfuls and shoved them into her duffel bag. A hand reached up from behind the desk and grabbed a fistful of her coat.

"You bitch," the Kijkaan gurgled. A fluid length of scales slid around the desk and dragged him away from her as he dug his nails into the mold on the floor. The pink sponge, now rosy and moisturized, pushed a pair of brown eyes up through the thick surface of its skin to rest below a thin membrane. A pair of teeth stretched open on the opposite end and the lump of dough dragged itself forward to chomp on Loisaida's tail. Nails grabbed it and tossed it to the back of the office.

A blast of fire turned their attention back to the Kijkaan. He pushed aside two blistered hunks of meat as Loisaida's torso contracted in pain.

"Get out," he commanded.

"No."

He turned to the group and pointed back down the hallway. "Out."

"Make us," Sam said, pulling a bone.

He hesitated briefly. "*Now.*"

Loisaida rose up from where she was crumpled on the floor and dragged him back down with her. They wrestled like children but froze when the door to the stairwell rattled loudly, as if something from outside were probing it for a grip.

The Kijkaan's eyes took on a wet, distant look.

"She's here. We have to go. Where's the ground-floor exit?" Loisaida asked.

He didn't answer.

She slapped his cheek. "Kijkaan!"

"It's outside, with the downwards stairs," Nails said.

"Fuck!" she roared, punching the wall.

"Is there any other exit?" Alex asked.

The Kijkaan didn't answer.

"Do you want to *die* for your stupid underground empire?" Loisaida shouted, ripping him out of Bonnie's hand to shake him by the collar.

"It's not mine," he said weakly.

"Focus! Focus! Do you want to die!?" she demanded. "How else can we get out?"

"There is no other exit," the Kijkaan moaned. "Woolworth's didn't plan on being attacked from below."

She slapped him. His face went rigid with shock, then grew angry, then sagged back into indifference.

"Come *on*! Do something!" she shouted. "You've been building tunnels for years, build one right here!"

"No."

"*What?*"

He gave her a look full of bitter pride. "*No.*"

"You *idiot!*" she roared.

A silence fell, and from the entrance, a small, brittle voice carried over.

"Comé apri presto?" Pirdunu wondered crankily, then abandoned the knob and pounded on the door. "I know you're in there!"

"Go talk to her," Nails told Loisaida.

"Yes," the Kijkaan said, smiling coldly. "You can handle her."

She glared at him.

"You gotta try," Nails said.

"I have a better idea," Loisaida said, and snaked her coils around the Kijkaan, squeezing around his shoulders. "Give me everyone and everything on the Lord Beneath council."

He hesitated, then closed his eyes. "I won't give you the board."

"Then you go down alone," she said. "Tell me I don't have enough evidence from the people in this room to the names in your drawers."

"I'll give you the backers," he said.

She paused. "What backers?"

"Think about it," he pressed. "This isn't my business. I've never done this before. I always had ideas, but I never had the connections or the money to put something like this together. How would I start? By going to the courthouse to tell them to tear it all down and start over? They'd rip me to shreds. This was a setup. Politics isn't my game."

"You should have known politics wasn't a game before you started," Loisaida answered.

He laughed. It was a light, carefree sound, more joyous than any other noise he'd made. He dug his fingers into the top of his bald head. "I'm sorry! There, I said it. How dare I try to be something I'm not. I wanted to help people. I never knew why politicians couldn't. My mistake! I'd never been behind the curtain."

"Do you think *I* am part of this conspiracy?" she asked dryly.

"It's not a conspiracy— I have all the proof I need to defend my position," the Kijkaan argued.

"Good. Where is it?"

"It's all here," he said. "All of it. You can have it! Take it!"

"I want the full story, first."

"I joined the team about four years ago," the Kijkaan explained. "But things were in the planning stages for years before that. I'm sure there were different iterations in development for centuries, maybe as long as there's been a Thundertown."

"That seems more proof to me that others tried and failed to keep track of New York's trasgo then that there's a conspiracy," Loisaida said.

"That's not the point," the Kijkaan snapped. "You need to listen to me. I didn't come to you with plans to overthrow the entire court system, I came to you with a bandage to cover a population in dire need of representation. That doesn't make me a dictator."

"Are you accepting responsibility for the management of the board of directors in the Lord Beneath?"

"No!" he shouted. "I'm not the boss! I'm the point of contact! I'm the middle man, I pass messages between the Board and the Backers! I sought out support because I couldn't do it alone, but the more we did, the less I contributed. The board members took care of their own territories, and the backers handed me practically everything else. They planned the particulars of the board's structure, our legal documentation, our charter— things I didn't even realize we needed arrived in my office complete and ready to be put into effect. When I saw how far out of my element I was, I took a less involved role and allowed others to go where they were needed. But then we left the planning stage and went into construction, the accidents began—"

"Are you trying to say those accidents weren't your fault either?" Nails asked.

"Yes! I was barely involved!" He cried.

"Fuck you," Alex spat.

"If it was so bad, why did you stay on the team?" Loisaida asked.

"Because we needed this!" he shouted. "You might have forgotten what it was like down here, but I used to shit in a spittoon. I still don't have drinking water. There are people under your territory who haven't had protection in nearly two hundred years. We could have given them every modern comfort the City can provide."

"All that good you were going to do, and you're still going to give me your backers."

"Yes," he cried. "Yes, yes, of course. We'll find other sponsors, re-plan our construction, secure the City's approval. It'll push us back a few years, but I'll do anything to avoid another mess."

"So this changes nothing, and you've learned nothing." Loisaida sighed.

"That's not *true*!" he cried, slamming his fists on the ground. "I know what I did wrong! I know I was out of my depth! I know I made mistakes!"

"I don't believe you," Loisaida said coldly.

OUTSIDE, PIRDUNU RATTLED the door like a storm. She called out to them with false promises of presents if they opened the door.

An orb of light sat in the middle, like a fire. Loisaida stared unblinking into its heart with her chin on a nest of coils. The Kijkaan passed quietly into sleep and snored quietly in the corner. When the others heard him snoring, they quickly realized Loisaida was sleeping, too, her eyelids open but pupils unfocused. The shifter curled up into a featureless lump under the side table. As the conversation died, they each found a patch of ground to stretch out on. They pushed the light behind a filing cabinet, where it burned down to a small red ball the size of a fist. Smoke issued from the floor beneath it.

"Maybe she'll forget about us and go home," Nails suggested.

"Yeah, maybe," Sam said without conviction.

THERE WAS NO morning. The night didn't slip quietly by, but came and went in bursts. They were shaken awake by banging on the door and inquisitive scratching. Pirdunu calling out plaintively to them, chattering nonsense about the beauty of the cavern, then roared in frustration.

"It's fine, the blocks are holding," the Kijkaan said when she promised she would be with them soon. Later they were awoken by a sharp snap, and he kicked Loisaida awake so she could release him. They both ran into the hallway as the air filled with the sound of wood cracking, and in the distance, they could hear the frustrated growls of a caged animal. When they returned, Loisaida tried again to make the Kijkaan open a tunnel in the office, but after some muttering about the logistics, he admitted that he was just as likely to collapse the cavern if he messed with it.

Much, much later, they woke one at a time and discovered there was no sound coming through the door.

They made their way slowly to the stairwell and listened at the door.

"I don't hear nothing," Nails whispered.

"She could be waiting to ambush us," Loisaida remarked. "One of us should go check."

Together they grabbed the Kijkaan and pushed him, kicking and screaming, out the door. They slammed it on his hands as he wailed and fed his fingers one by one through the crack, then listened as he hammered on the door, howling plaintively.

He fell silent, except for the ragged gasps of panic. His footsteps crept towards the stairs with little, gasping whimpers. Then there was nothing. Before they could decide whether they should open the door, he ran back and pounded on the door.

"She's here! She's here! Let me in!"

They opened the door to grab him at the same time Pirdunu jumped on him, carrying him through the doorway and down the hallway with his throat in her teeth. She looked up with a satisfied roll of her shoulders, and the Kijkaan's throat erupted in blood.

Loisaida managed a shaky smile. "Buonasera, Signora."

"Buongiorno," she agreed, licking her lips.

"Do you know who I am?"

"Si, Picchina Onorinna," she said in a sing-song voice. "Al-Hasan's great hope for the future."

"I have taken over his title," Loisaida said slowly. "His responsibilities are mine."

Pirdunu didn't seem to be listening but savoring the taste in her mouth with great satisfaction.

"I am afraid—" Loisaida stopped, then started again. "I'm afraid you've attacked someone under my protection."

Pirdunu screwed up her nose and shook her head. "No."

"Yes."

"No."

"He's right there, Pirdunu."

She looked down at the Kijkaan. "This is?"

"We can debate this in court."

She laughed. "Court! Jiri a lettu! What can those cowards do to me?"

The Kijkaan rolled on his belly with a wet gurgle.

Loisaida focused her eyes on him. "I need to reach that man, Donna."

She looked down. "Tutti manciamu, picchina."

"Come on, Donna," Loisaida cooed. Behind the shield of her back, Sam passed one of her bones to Alex.

Loisaida tried one last time to make Pirdunu consent to healing the Kijkaan. She moved forward half a foot. Rather than stand down, Pirdunu tensed.

"Look—" she said casually, then dove toward his prone body. Pirdunu sank her teeth into her side as she passed, but before she could land another blow, Sam slammed her club into the floor and sliced the air with an arc of fire. The spear tip landed in the wall, missing Pirdunu entirely, but the blade of lightning didn't die. It flickered, trying to dissipate into the cold, dry air, but kept alive by the little figure in the white dress pushing it into Pirdunu's side.

It made contact with her in a flashing strobe. Pirdunu's head seemed to lift in slow motion as she screamed. Smoke filled the cavern and the light died, but

Pirdunu's screams still rang through the cavern. The lightning's entry point burnt her hip to a cinder and left forks of raw flesh to branch across her back.

The sight, the smell, the blood; it was all overwhelming. Alex took two steps forward with his club and faltered, backing away from the screaming old woman.

Loisaida had one hand on the wound in her side and the other on the Kijkaan's neck, struggling to close the gap. His hands and arms moved as if trying to swim.

Alex heard his name, which brought him back to Pirdunu as she tried to stand, still screaming. All he could see was her teeth, but one sharp eye appeared and focused on him.

Her hand whipped forward and a bolt of fire shot through the air towards him. Before he could choose to dodge it, Lucinda caught it. He ran straight through her like a mist and brought the bone down.

"No!" Loisaida screamed.

Pirdunu did not dodge. She watched him come at her with her mouth open.

The force of the thunder crushed her skull in one blow. He was covered in a spray of meat and blood, shards of bone striking his face like glass.

Pirdunu stiffened, shat, and fell to the ground. He dropped the bone. Sam was at his back in an instant and turned him around, away from what he'd done.

Loisaida broke the silence with a sharp inhale. She circled Pirdunu's body, as if she wanted to touch her, but instead pressed her face into the wall and wailed.

Alex clapped his hands over his ears. His heart was pounding in his chest.

Nails skipped around them all to check the Kijkaan's pulse, then grabbed him by the armpits and lift him to his feet.

"You tried to kill me," the Kijkaan said dumbly.

Nails patted him on the shoulder and steered him to the door. "We should go."

The others agreed. Even the Kijkaan nodded, faintly, while his fingers walked over and between the holes torn through his collar.

"Alex?"

The cold fever running over his body broke into sudden nausea. "I need to sit."

"We can sit later," Nails insisted. "Let's go. We have to go. Miss LES, please—"

He managed to push the whole group out onto the stairwell, but there, the group dynamic broke. Loisaida collapsed and wailed her heart out, while Alex took a seat on the stairs and quietly lost track of time.

SOMETIME LATER, LOISAIDA stopped crying abruptly. She sniffled and turned around to face the Kijkaan. "Tell me who set you up."

He didn't answer.

"Do you want your deal or not?" she demanded. His eyes skipped one by one over all of their faces, calculating, then back to her torso. There was a new, calculating focus to his eyes.

After a period of silence, Nails spoke. "It was that NGO—the Bureau."

All eyes turned on him.

He fidgeted self-consciously. "It makes sense, right? He said it couldn't be the City because he never worked with them before and because they don't want to step on the courts, because they have a good thing going between them right now. But it's not the courts, because— well, he said it. But it's not nobody, because he literally couldn't do it by himself. So who else is there? They're in the business, but they're not on a side. They can organize, but they can't build anything, 'cause they don't have builders. And 'cause they're not on a side, they don't have land deeds or court documents—"

"—but they know who does," Loisaida finished. "And they're the only org still operating that's been trying to map Thundertown for a long enough time to make it feasible."

"The Thunder Tunnels had electricity and garbage cans when we went there," Alex said, thinking back to that wide, tall space that was more like a government project than any bolthole he'd ever seen. The garbage cans really struck him; not even his mother's neighborhood had public trash pickup.

Loisaida slowly drew her lip between her teeth, then released it with a small pop. "That would be a very heavy case to carry, and I'm not sure— but we'll see what his paper trail reveals and build a case from there."

The Kijkaan looked up sharply. "Our deal—"

"It's still in place," she promised, advancing up the stairs. "Clemency for you and your board members. I'll send someone to go through your files. We'll need to petition all the courts in order to process you, and I can't think right now which State Court this would go to— god, what an awful night."

She chattered to herself all the way to the top, stopping abruptly at the brick ceiling. One by one, all eyes turned to the Kijkaan.

"Well?" Loisaida demanded. "Open it."

He opened his palm, and something changed, but instead of the entrance appearing above them, the gun in Bonnie's pocket, holster and all, nestled into his hand. He removed the holster and unclipped the safety with a tight smile.

Bonnie bared her teeth. "That's *mine*!"

He showed teeth in an anxious grimace. He pulled the trigger.

It let out a dry click, and nothing more.

While he was staring at the gun, Bonnie struck him across the face and sent him first into the banister, then rolling back down the stairs to come to a halt at the bottom.

Epilogue

THE INITIAL INQUIRY did not cause a sensation; Loisaida and the Kijkaan presented their case side by side, their lawyers each carrying folios of collated and stapled documents to verify their claims. The review happened behind closed doors, without media attention. The Bureau sent an attorney to defend them, and once the judge reviewed both cases, she decided to let it go to court.

Neither did the first few trials catch more than cursory attention. Local outlets put them on the front page for a day, then let the story drop.

Sam, Cassandra, and Leticia were called to speak, followed by the Card House tenants, the owners of the plot under the FDR, and first responders to the Avenue D accident. A group of people who had to be lifted out of the side of the riverbed, and their rescuers, came forward. And then, when the tone of the case was about to be decided, the Kijkaan did an about-face and sued Loisaida, Sam, and Nails, for aggravated assault and attempted homicide.

A MONTH AFTER crawling out of the fire exit behind the Home Depot, Nails came back to Staten Island with three sealed envelopes.

Alex last saw Nails weeks earlier as dawn made the sky iridescent. The alarm at the Home Depot was still going off while they all gathered on the sidewalk.

"I'm not going to Staten Island," Nails said, frowning at the sky. "Staten Island's too far away for me."

Since then, Nails found every excuse not to visit. It could have been for a simple desire to stay connected with the rest of the City, or for the freedom to sleep on his own bed, but privately, Alex felt like it was because of something he did.

Now Nails was back, with three envelopes spread out on the couch as if nothing was wrong.

"Did you see ATAKK while they were in town?" he asked, knowing Alex wasn't at the show. "They were great. Josh built a pyramid out of empties and jumped through it."

Alex opened his envelope and found a formal invitation to Donna Purdunu's funeral on cream cardstock.

"Packrat tried to get in, but the bouncer didn't like his ID," Nails added.

Alex wasn't listening. There on the invite was Purdunu's true name, Yasmin Artemu-Anapia du Centuluci-al-Hasan. There was even more after that, listing titles of lordship over places Alex never heard of and couldn't pronounce.

"Loisaida told me to give it to you," Nails said about the envelope, watching Alex read the invitation.

There were two more envelopes on the table. One of them was clearly for Nails, but he couldn't figure out who should get the last one. Not Sam, since she would have seen Loisaida in person.

Nails looked away when Alex tried to meet his eyes.

"For your mother," he explained.

He imagined Loisaida planning the funeral, the flowers and coffin, making a guest list, and pausing after writing down his name. He wanted to shred the invitation. Maybe if he said nothing, the envelope would stay there until after the funeral. He imagined his mother picking it up one morning on her next day off, as she gathered the mail that was delivered throughout the week and scattered around the house. She'd read it at arm's length, squinting through her glasses, then find him standing nearby and ask what it meant. He could tell her it was nothing, and it would pass like it was nothing.

But there was a challenge in the invitation that he couldn't ignore. As much as he didn't want his mother to see him as a murderer, it was a gentler punishment than he deserved. It was a question; would he take responsibility for what he'd done? There would be no consequences if he didn't.

He took her invitation upstairs as Nails watched and knocked on the door.

She took the envelope, opened it, and read it— at arms' length, with a frown. When she was done, she took off her glasses. "What is this?"

"It's a funeral invitation," he said.

"I can tell. Who is it from? Did I know this woman?"

He shook his head. "I did."

That's all he could bring himself to say. Natalia made an impatient noise and put the invitation face-down on the bed, carefully separated from her other paperwork.

He went back down the stairs, took a seat at the dining room table, and put his head in his hands.

About the Author

O F Cieri is a novelist and amateur historian in New York City. Lord of Thundertown is her first novel.

Her work examines the lifelong effects of trauma, grief and poverty through the exaggerated lens of the supernatural. She draws from contemporary horror to magnify her plots' conflict with surreal elements.

She collects art, insects, and antiques.

Email: obfvscate@gmail.com

Facebook: www.facebook.com/obfvscate

Twitter: @obfvscate

Website: www.ofcieri.com

Also Available from NineStar Press

Connect with NineStar Press

www.ninestarpress.com

www.facebook.com/ninestarpress

www.facebook.com/groups/NineStarNiche

www.twitter.com/ninestarpress

www.tumblr.com/blog/ninestarpress